**"Pete, I appreciate your offer to help, but God will take care of me,"**

Sunny said.

Pete's eyes lifted innocently. "You don't think God uses people to carry out His plans? For all you know, I could be your guardian angel in disguise."

Sunny laughed at the thought. Would God send her a handsome charmer, especially when He knew how much she didn't trust them?

Then again, Pete *could* be an angel, the way he made her feel that her problems were tiny and that contentment was fingertip near.

But Pete Maguire looked nothing like any storybook angel she'd ever seen. Not with that lock of black hair falling over his brow, the wicked half smile and the teasing gleam in his eyes.

If Pete really was her guardian angel...

...that was some disguise!

**Books by Patt Marr**

Love Inspired

*Angel in Disguise #98*

## PATT MARR

has a friend who says she reminds him of a car that's either zooming along in the fast lane or sitting on the shoulder, out of gas. Her family says he's dead right.

At age twenty she had a B.S. in business education, a handsome, good-hearted husband and a sweet baby girl. Since then, Patt, a professional musician, has earned an M.A. in counseling, worked a lifetime as a high school educator, cooked big meals for friends, attended a zillion basketball games where her husband coached and her son played, and enjoyed many years of church music, children's ministries, drama and television productions.

In down time, Patt reads romances, eats too much chocolate, watches too many movies and sleeps way too little. She's been blessed with two darling granddaughters, wonderful friends, a great church and a chance to write love stories about people who love God as much as she does.

# Angel in Disguise
## Patt Marr

Love Inspired®

Published by Steeple Hill Books™

STEEPLE HILL BOOKS

Steeple
Hill™

ISBN 0-373-87104-X

ANGEL IN DISGUISE

Copyright © 2000 by Patt Marr

Visit us at www.steeplehill.com

**Printed in U.S.A.**

Trust in the Lord and do good...and He shall give
you the desires of your heart.

—*Psalms* 37:3-4

For a first book, there are many people to thank for their encouragement and support: family, friends, the Romance Writers of America, teachers of the craft and most of all, God. Special thanks go to my husband, David Marr, for sharing his knowledge of basketball coaching and providing many pots of coffee, to Randall McNaughton, Eldon Partridge and Big Bear Rangers for sharing their knowledge of camping and hiking, and to Medical Arts physicians for providing information about the character Pete Maguire.

I dedicate this first book to J-J
My wonderful, precious daughter

# *Prologue*

Sunny Keegan stepped inside the sanctuary three hours before her wedding wearing well-washed jeans, a faded yellow T-shirt and comfortable sneakers. The clothes felt just right, but the headpiece to her bridal veil had either been pinned too tightly or she was unbelievably tense.

She touched her temples, wishing she could massage circles there, but that wouldn't do. She might smudge her professionally applied makeup and she'd already made the mistake of wearing a T-shirt to have her hair done. Someone would have to scissor her free, and that was a shame for the old shirt held great memories. She'd put it on today, wanting to wear something familiar, something of her own. This wedding sure wasn't.

Not that she was complaining. If things had gotten out of hand, it was her own fault for letting her mother and the wedding consultant run with the ball. But, as her father said, she was her mother's only daughter, and it was true her parents' wealth could handle any extravagance. Even for a Beverly Hills wedding, though, some of the plans were over the top.

The dove release, for instance, was extreme, and the twenty-limousine caravan pure ostentation. What her parents were paying for flowers could have housed the homeless, and the price of her beaded wedding gown, six inches longer than Princess Di's had been, could have fed them. Their two thousand guests certainly didn't need a seven-course dinner, and one band was enough, not three.

Since her groom had objected to none of it, she'd let things slide. She couldn't blame Bruce for appreciating what he called "the good life" since it wasn't something he had known all his life.

She looked down the long aisle and tried to imagine him standing beside his nine attendants and herself beside her own nine, all of them dressed in white. White didn't particularly flatter her redhead's coloring, but it was supposed to make an elegant June wedding.

Bruce, with his dark hair and eyes, would look fantastic in white. He had such presence, such charisma. All eyes would be on him, and that was fine with her. Handsome, well educated, successful, Bruce was perfect. Even her parents thought so. Finally she'd done something right. That this wonderful man loved her as much as she loved him seemed almost a miracle. But he loved her. There was no doubt about it.

So why was she standing here with lead in her

stomach and a sinking heart? She might as well admit it, she'd give anything if she could run.

*Lord, if this is just prewedding jitters, please ease my spirit. Give me the joy of a bride on her wedding day. If this is anything else, then I ask that You give me a sign, an unmistakable sign. As much as I love Bruce, as much as my parents would be upset, I would walk away from all this if it's not what You want. I can't imagine You letting me get this far without it being Your will, but I should know better than question. In all things, I trust You.*

Sunny took a deep breath and realized she felt better. Prayer always helped. She'd been silly, imagining some dark foreboding, wasting time when she should find the changing room and let the bridal staff go to work, transforming her into a beautiful bride. Her mother swore they could do wonders.

At both ends of the foyer, stairs led to a lower level where the changing rooms were. The women's area was supposed to be at one end, off a courtyard centered with an angel fountain, and the men were on the opposite side. Exactly where she wasn't sure because she hadn't been paying attention during the wedding coordinator's instructions. She couldn't, not with Bruce kissing her neck, whispering "babe" in her ear. He knew how she loved that.

Uncertain which end of the foyer to choose, she tried the left stairs, and was relieved when she spotted a bubbling fountain centered with angels—well, to be precise, cherubs, but people often said one when they meant the other. She was probably in the right place, and it would only take a minute to check.

If she was wrong, the worst that could happen was Bruce teasing her about her sense of direction. Knowing him, he'd steal a kiss and walk her back. How bad could that be?

The rooms around the courtyard were laid out in a circular design, and the first one, a small reception area, had obviously been claimed by the florist. The second was a bookstore, dark and closed at this hour. The third opened into a small library, also dark, but voices came from inside. She walked into the carpeted room and discovered an alcove tucked under the stairs with two chairs and a large sofa, its back toward her.

Two people lay on the sofa. She smiled to herself. They were so wrapped up in each other, they didn't even know she was here. If she retreated, quiet as a mouse, she'd be gone before they realized their privacy had been invaded. Why they'd chosen this place and this time for a tryst, she couldn't imagine, but it was none of her business. Today she wished all lovers well.

She had almost returned to the checkout desk when she heard the woman moan a name. Every muscle in her body tightened. Her heart nearly stopped.

"Bruce," the woman moaned again. "This is crazy."

Slowly Sunny turned, her eyes focused on that sofa, her hearing on the couple's passionate breathing, their murmured words. It sounded like Bruce and the bridesmaid she barely knew, a distant cousin of his whom he'd wanted as a member of their wedding party.

Inch by inch, she retraced her steps, drawn by a desperate need to prove she was wrong, until she stood so near they should have sensed her presence. They would have if they hadn't been oblivious to everything but each other. Watching them, disillusionment clawed at her soul.

"We shouldn't be doing this, Bruce, especially not here, not now," the woman murmured.

"You worry too much. It's okay, babe."

Babe? That's what Bruce always called her.

"But what if someone walks in on us?" the woman argued.

"That's half the fun, knowing there's the off chance it could happen. But the guys aren't due for another hour, and the women are on the other side of the church."

"Where I'm supposed to be," the woman said with a giggle.

"But not yet. There's plenty of time before we have to be dressed for the pictures." He kissed the woman's neck, and she giggled again.

Horrified, Sunny stared, not believing something this awful could happen. Nausea curled in waves of revulsion. She couldn't breathe, couldn't think.

"Wait until you see me in my bridesmaid dress."

"I'd rather see you out of it."

She'd never heard Bruce talk that way. A sleazy lounge lizard had more finesse.

The woman giggled again. "Bruce! You are so naughty!"

"But you like it," he teased, kissing the hollow spot at the base of her neck until her laughter turned into a moan.

"Oh, babe," he murmured, "I don't think I could get through this fiasco with Li'l Sunshine if it weren't for you."

This had to be a terrible, hideous dream. Please, God, let her wake and escape it.

"I love it when you do that," the woman said with a sigh.

"If you liked that, how about this?"

Tears burned behind Sunny's eyes. She'd never had Bruce's love. Not if he could do this. It had all been a sham. How humiliating to know he'd made such a fool of her.

Then again, humiliation was a choice. It didn't have to be hers. Not today. Not ever. He didn't have to know how devastated she felt, how belittled.

Her heart pounding, she shook his shoulder roughly. "Bruce," she said, getting his attention.

He looked up, and the shock on his face should have been satisfying, but she was too shattered to care.

"Sunny!" He pushed away from the woman. "This is not what it seems." Caught red-handed, he lied as he buttoned his shirt.

"I think it's exactly what it seems." Betrayal like this was hard to disguise.

He raked his hand though his hair. "I can explain."

How stupid did he think she was? She met his eyes boldly, contempt coursing through her body. "Just pretend I was never here. I'll lock the door on my way out so no one else will disturb you. Take your time. There's no rush, not anymore, for the wedding is off."

"No!" He reached toward her, his eyes wide with alarm.

It was a first, seeing fear on his face.

"You know I love you, Sunny!"

Oh, she could see that.

"C'mon, Sunny, don't be this way." Tucking in his shirt, he rose from the sofa and came toward her.

She stopped him with a open palm. "Forget it!"

"But you've got to at least give me a chance, babe."

"Babe?" Fire-hot fury made her voice shrill. "Oh, no! I'm 'Li'l Sunshine.' Wasn't that it? Really, Bruce, you've got to do a better job of keeping your women straight. Here, let me help you."

She twisted the diamond from her finger and threw it at him, taking grim pleasure when it landed hard on his chin. "Now you have one less to worry about."

"Sunny! This isn't like you!"

It wasn't? Had she been a gullible fool all along?

"Sunny, darling, please…" His dark eyes were as beguiling as a puppy dog's, pleading for a better home than the pound. "Let's talk about this."

He actually believed he could turn this around? Did he think that much of himself or that little of her?

"Just give me a minute, darling. I can make this okay."

"Sorry. Time's up." Pivoting, she ran from the room.

"Sunny! Wait!"

She heard him following her and panicked. She'd left with some measure of dignity, but she'd taken as much as she could. He must not see these hot, renegade tears spilling down her cheeks, but where could she go?

*Lord, tell me what to do.*

In front of her were glass double doors marked with red letters. The message read Exit, and that's what she did.

# Chapter One

*Eight months later*

Sweat trickled down Pete Maguire's back as he stood behind a pulsing neon heart and listened to the studio audience applaud the last contestant's entrance. It was the last time his little sister would catch him coming to her rescue. If Meggy couldn't handle her new job as a *Dream Date* production assistant, she could broil burgers somewhere. Setting him up to appear on national television was the last straw.

He shifted his shoulders and tried to get comfortable in the clothes she'd provided when she dragged him out of the house as a last-minute replacement. He'd have to talk to her about her taste in ties. Real men did not wear grapes and leafy things.

With his heart pounding as loud as it was, he barely heard the show's host say, ''The last of our contestants is a guy named Pete.'' That was his cue

to go on, and he'd do it if his body would cooperate.
Someone shoved the middle of his back and he
stepped into blinding bright light.

"Pete, a carpenter by trade, says he's looking for
a girl just like Mom."

A carpenter. If they only knew. Well, it was true
enough once. And more accurate than anything else
these days, unless you wanted to count rich, worthless beach bum. Though nearly blinded, he headed
toward the one unoccupied chair on the set. A spon-
taneous scream from the women in the audience
startled him. For his sister's sake, he tried to look
pleased and threw the audience a wave. They
screamed again. Man, Meggy owed him big.

"Welcome, Pete! It's going to be a great show,
folks!" the host proclaimed. "After we break for
commercial, we're going to match one lovely lady
with one lucky guy and send them on their very own
*Dream Date!* Don't go 'way."

Pete settled into his leather chair and checked out
the group. The guy next to him was a regular weight
lifter. If the sleeveless T-shirt showcasing massive
biceps didn't give him away, the tree-trunk neck did.

The other guy had longer hair than most women,
holes in his jeans, a dangly earring and a soulful
look. Two bucks said he played a guitar and
screamed into a mic.

Pete fingered his ugly tie. He could have worn
what he wore at the beach and felt less out of place
here. Leave it to a woman to overdress a guy.

The three female contestants were knockouts. The
lush blonde was giving him the eye, and the petite
brunette looked unbelievably interested, as well.

Pete wondered which they liked best—his new nose, cheekbones or chin.

He still wasn't used to The Face, as he'd come to call it, or women's reaction to it. He doubted if he ever would be. No matter how much the guys with knives changed his looks, he was the same Pete Maguire he'd been for thirty-two years.

There'd been a time he'd have appreciated two babes checking him out. Shoot, he'd have been tickled with one. You'd think a guy whose wife had dumped him for his best friend would be happy with the attention, but that wasn't the way it worked. Not when he knew it wasn't him that turned them on— just The Face.

The redhead across from him seemed preoccupied with covering long, gorgeous legs with a skimpy black leather skirt. From the way she flipped that mane of coppery curls, he'd say she'd give a lot to be just about anywhere else. Edgy, that's what she was. Real edgy. And indifferent to him. Good for her.

Signaling the end of the commercial, the stage manager pointed to the show's host who smiled at a camera and said, "It's time for our guys and gals to share their responses to our *Dream Date* questionnaire. When a gal's answer matches a guy's, they get a matchmaker point. Everybody understand?"

Pete understood the questionnaire was a big deal, but Meggy said she'd completed his with such crazy answers he couldn't possibly win. Thirty minutes, she'd said, and it would be over.

"Okay, here we go," the host said. "Remember,

the couple with the most points at the end of the show shares a fabulous *Dream Date*. Then in a couple of weeks they'll return to rate their date. Will it be a dream...or a nightmare? Everybody ready?''

Pete hadn't dated since high school and wasn't about to start now. He leaned forward in his chair, the better to concentrate on losing.

"The first category," host Mike Michaels enthused, "is 'Food on a First Date.' On their bios, contestants were asked to state where or what sort of food they would enjoy on a *Dream Date*. Cheryl," he said to the blonde with the low neckline, "let's start with you. What's your choice in food?"

"Well, Mike, I like really nice restaurants. Romantic places with gourmet food and fine wine. Oh, and valet parking."

The audience chuckled, and Pete smiled at the idea of turning his old pickup over to a parking attendant. ELEGANT DINING popped onto the board behind the woman. Mike moved on to the brunette. "Jacy, how about you?"

"Sushi, Mike. Can't get enough sushi. I like to head down to the marina and spend some time there."

As SUSHI appeared on the electronic board behind Jacy, Pete wondered if either the weight lifter or the longhair were more willing to eat raw fish than he was.

Mike turned to the redhead. "Sunny, what's your preference?"

Sunny glanced at the studio audience where a

dozen or so teenage girls chanted, "Do it. Do it. Do it."

Taking a deep breath, she turned back to the emcee and said, "Mike, I like to stay home and cook for my dates."

Looks could be deceiving, but Pete would have bet his pickup that this woman didn't know a whisk from a blender.

The board faithfully registered HOME COOKING, and the host looked at the redhead with awe. "We don't get too many women choosing to cook. Bet you're real popular, Sunny."

The redhead grinned and shrugged her shoulders. Personality sparkled in her pretty brown eyes.

It was only a little twinge Pete felt. A little zing in the gut. But it took him by surprise. It had been so long since it happened that a moment passed before he recognized the feeling. Attraction, he guessed you'd call it. Man, it had been a while.

Even in the old days he'd never been attracted to redheads, yet he felt the impact of this one's smile right down to his socks. What was her name? Sunny? She sure was when she smiled. The smile was beautiful. In fact, spectacular.

She caught him staring at her. Her eyes were huge, the warm color of butternut, and uneasy. Rather pointedly, she turned toward the host. He had to smile. She didn't know it, but she didn't have to worry about him coming on to her. Any interest he had in her was purely analytical.

"Kevin," Mike said to the longhair, "on your questionnaire you stated that you prefer ethnic food. Right?"

"Mostly Mexican and Thai. The hotter the better," Kevin claimed in a dark, sultry voice, dramatically swishing his hair as ETHNIC FOODS registered.

Pete was fairly sure he'd have trouble relating to Kevin.

"Frank, our fireman from the LAFD..."

"Firefighter," the weight lifter corrected politely.

"Frank the firefighter," the emcee repeated good-naturedly, "says he prefers pasta and salad. Looks good on you, Frank."

Frank smiled as if he might think so, too. Pete approved of his diet, if not the attitude.

"According to Pete," the host said, "the perfect meal is a big pot roast, mashed potatoes and gravy, corn on the cob dripping with butter and chocolate-chip cheesecake."

The audience groaned. So did Pete, at least inwardly. He avoided red meat and kept an eye on his fat grams. The pot-roast fantasy was Meggy's creation. "Trust me," she'd said. "I know these girls and what they say."

She'd better, since her life was on the line.

"Pete also says," continued the host, "that his favorite place to eat is his mom's own backyard. Isn't that nice?"

The audience laughed. Pete thought they'd get an even bigger kick if they knew his mother was so into her art that she never knew when it was time to eat.

He looked warily at the board behind Sunny. Her HOME COOKING could be a match with Frank's PASTA or the POT ROAST hanging over his own head.

"What do you say, audience?" yelled the host.

"Which couple matches? Cast your electronic votes now."

In mere seconds the boards flashed behind Pete and Sunny.

The "Do it" girls exploded in screams and piercing whistles as they high-fived each other all over the place. The blonde threw him a pout, and the brunette seemed disappointed.

Sunny looked as if she'd been sentenced to ten days in the county jail. He wasn't happy about the match, either, but he couldn't say he liked her reaction.

In the second category, which had to go better than the first, Mike started with the guys, asking their music preference on a first date. Frank the firefighter liked rhythm and blues. Kevin the longhair predictably talked about rock and said he sang with a band. Since Pete didn't know the answer Meggy had given for him, he gave his honest preference: country.

Sunny's answer, "All types of music," made him nervous until Cheryl answered, "Rock." That, of course, was a perfect match with Kevin the longhair, and Pete breathed easier.

For the next category, "TV Preference on a First Date," Mike started with Sunny. "I understand you're a teacher and the girls' basketball coach at San Josita High?"

She nodded and flashed that beautiful, warm smile. Again Pete felt the zing, and again it surprised him.

Mike glanced out at the teenagers. "You didn't happen to bring the team with you?"

"Whuh, whuh, whuh," the group of girls chanted.

"Actually, Mike, they brought me. This was their idea. I promised to do anything they wanted if they'd win the regional championship. They won."

"Get a nice trophy?"

"Big trophy. Huge," she said, smiling down at the girls.

"Congratulations! I can see you're proud of your team, and it looks as if they're rooting for you to take home a 'huge' trophy from *Dream Date.*"

The audience laughed, especially when the firefighter flexed a bicep. The girls broke out more high fives. Pete frowned. He couldn't see Sunny and the firefighter together, but what did he know? Or care.

"What kind of TV do you watch on a first date, Sunny?"

"Sports. Football or basketball, mostly."

Pete's mouth went dry. If he were honest, that's what he'd say, too. But hey, all guys would. Well, maybe not the longhair, but he knew he could depend on the firefighter.

Kevin's answer, MTV, and Frank's SPORTS, came as no surprise. His own preference, again compliments of Meggy, was a revelation. He was sure he had never watched SPORT FISHING. In fact, he wouldn't know a trout from a tuna, but he had to give Meggy credit. It put him in the clear. He smiled as the match went to Frank and Sunny.

Not only was her team ecstatic, Sunny didn't seem to mind winning this one. If he'd cared, he might have taken the difference in her reaction personally.

In the category "Transportation on a First Date," it was a tie. Jacy the brunette matched Kevin with FOREIGN SPORTS CAR, and for their second point, Sunny matched Pete with PICKUP TRUCK.

It was true that more women drove pickups these days, but he couldn't imagine this redhead in her miniskirt behind the wheel of one.

"Congrats on your second point, Pete and Sunny!" The emcee beamed at them. "What do you think, Sunny? Have you got a place on your mantel for a trophy like Pete?"

Sunny forced herself to laugh along with the audience even though there was positively no place in her life for a state-of-the-art stud like Pete. He reminded her so much of Bruce, it was scary. Give her an average-looking, good-hearted guy anyday, not some blue-eyed, raven-haired hunk.

During the next break, she waved at her girls and tried to act as if she were having a good time. She loved those kids, and, more than anything, wanted them to love the Lord. Sometimes it made it hard for her to be as firm with them as she should.

For instance, she should have put her foot down when they claimed dressing her for the show was part of the deal. Tugging on this dinky strip of leather they called a skirt, trying to gain an inch of modesty, she thought of her family's reaction. Daddy's blood pressure would soar, and Mother would choke on her pearls.

She didn't especially like the idea of upsetting them, but maybe they'd finally realize she wasn't going back to Bruce, no matter how much he promised to win her. Last month he'd gone too far, showing up at her school, announcing she was his fiancée and ruining the relative anonymity she'd enjoyed this school year. Now, faculty and students alike believed Bruce's version, and the rumor mill was killing her.

But her girls knew her and smelled a rat. If she were engaged they'd have known it. Why Bruce would pretend something that wasn't true, they didn't know, but they knew it wasn't right.

Behind her back, they'd set her up for this show. Her ex couldn't claim he was engaged to a *Dream Date* contestant, could he? It made sense to her. So here she was, rooting for the women beside her, counting the minutes until the show ended.

In the new round, "Outdoor Activity on a First Date," the guy with the earring said he liked to walk along the beach, and the guy with the bull neck said he liked mountain climbing. Hopefully she wouldn't get matched with anyone, but if she absolutely had to be matched, she prayed it would be with one of them. They didn't intimidate her at all. Just please not the hunk. Though he did have the sweetest smile she'd ever seen, she wanted no part of him. Guys like him were so full of themselves; they did what they pleased and expected you to thank them for it. She'd already been there and done that.

He must have felt her eyes on him for he slid one of his slow, lopsided smiles her way. Warm tingles fluttered in her stomach, and she almost smiled back. Silly tingles, reacting to chemistry instead of good sense.

"Pete," the emcee said, "tell us about being a carpenter. What kind of carpentry do you do?"

A strange look crossed Pete's face. Then he gave Mike a phony smile. Definitely phony. She was an expert on that. It was an odd reaction to a simple question.

"Mostly residential construction," he said.

It wasn't exactly the truth. She was sure of it, but why lie about that?

"Your questionnaire says your choice of 'Outdoor Activity on a First Date' is camping and exploring the great outdoors. How long have you been into 'exploring the great outdoors'?"

The guy glanced uneasily toward the side of the stage. It wasn't the first time Sunny had noticed an interchange between him and a cute brunette holding a clipboard.

"Mike," he said, clearing his throat, "I can't remember when I first became interested in camping and…exploring, but it's been…an indescribable part of my life."

Even without her teaching experience, Sunny recognized hooey when she heard it. Why had he made that up?

Pete's lack of candor apparently didn't bother Cheryl, the first woman in the round, for she sent a seductive glance his way and said to the emcee, "Mike, I know my bio says my favorite outdoor activity is shopping, but I want to change that to camping and exploring."

The audience laughed, but Pete looked embarrassed, which surprised her.

The host smiled regretfully. "'Fraid that's not the way it works, Cheryl. Let's see SHOPPING on Cheryl's scoreboard!"

Jacy's answer was "volleyball," and, for once, Sunny could answer honestly. The team had allowed her the one genuine preference. As she answered, and BACKPACKING went on the board, she knew why. Backpacking had point-maker potential.

Mike instructed the audience, "Okay, ladies and gentlemen. We're down to the wire. Kevin has matched two of the women—Cheryl and Jacy. Sunny has matched two of the guys—once with Frank and *twice* with Pete. That means we could have a tie between Jacy and Sunny. Cheryl, honey, it looks like you'll have to go shopping alone, at least this time."

"That's okay," she said. "I had a great time. And, Pete, I'll give you my number. For a real date, you give me a call."

The crowd loved it. Sunny thought they made a perfect pair.

"Okay, what's it going to be, folks? Do you see Kevin and Jacy 'walking on the beach' after a hot game of 'volleyball'?"

"Oooo," the audience reacted. They had Sunny's vote.

"Or do you see Sunny 'backpacking' as she 'mountain climbs' with Frank? Or Sunny 'backpacking' as she 'camps and explores' with Pete?"

Sunny cringed as she heard far more people screaming her name and Pete's. Hot color crept up her neck. *Please, God, get me out of this.*

"A match for Sunny and Pete gives them a clear win. Otherwise we go into our tie-breaker. Okay, folks, time to cast your vote. Do it now."

Sunny heard her team chanting Pete's name and

thought of the windsprints and laps those girls would get.

When the scoreboards behind her and Pete registered the win, her heart sank. She didn't know how she was going to get out of this, but she was not going camping with a stranger.

Pete couldn't remember ever letting his sister down, but there had to be a first for everything. He wasn't doing the date.

"I can't do it, Meggy," he said, his arms folded, ready for the inevitable wheedling debate. "That wasn't part of our deal."

"I know. I don't expect you to."

That surprised him. From babyhood, she'd expected him to leap tall buildings if that was what it took to get her way.

"I'd like to help you out, but…"

"It's okay. A promise is a promise. I said you wouldn't have to do the date if you won, and you won't."

"You won't get into trouble?"

"It doesn't matter. I can always get another job."

Guilt was an awful thing to swallow. This was the best job Meggy had ever had. She loved this job.

"Who would have thought we'd get a woman who wanted to cook for her dates?" she muttered. "Ridiculous!"

Well, not from a man's point of view. That is, if he actually wanted a date.

She sighed, brave disappointment on her face. "That's it, then."

If he screwed this up for her, could he forgive himself? Probably not.

"I guess no job's perfect." She sighed again.

It was only one date. He could do it. Drawing an extra deep breath, he said, "Okay, you win, but don't expect me to bail you out again. This is the last time, understood?"

"You'll...do the date?" She looked stunned.

No wonder. He felt stunned. Already he could kick himself for rescuing her again. "What do I have to do?"

"I can't believe this," she whispered. A tear welled in her eye. "You haven't dated since..."

"Don't start. Just tell me what I have to do."

"Thank you, Pete," she said in a shaky voice as a tear dropped on her cheek.

"Darn it, Meggy, stop that." She knew he couldn't stand tears. He rubbed the tear away with his thumb.

She sniffed and gave him the watery smile she'd perfected as a toddler. "We'd better go meet the guy who plans the dates."

He followed Meggy down one hallway and then another, wondering what other guy would feel sick to his stomach knowing he had a date with a gorgeous redhead. A real, honest-to-goodness date. Time alone with a woman when you weren't sure what you were going to say or what was going to happen?

From junior high on, he'd been paired with Lisa. He'd never had to plan where they were going or what they'd do. Well, that much wouldn't change. *Dream Date* would take care of the planning.

He knew they were getting close to the meeting room when the girls' basketball team spotted him and started up that stupid "Pete, Pete, Pete" thing again. The piercing whistles came from the tallest girl. Pete had to respect the way she could whistle with her fingers in her mouth. He'd have given a baseball card to be able to do that when he'd been a kid.

In a conference room Sunny sat on a short sofa, showing more leg than she wanted if you judged by the way she shifted around, tugging at that little skirt. As far as Pete was concerned, she might as well give in gracefully. Those were truly great legs.

As he entered the room, the first thing he noticed was the change in Sunny. Her wide-eyed, admiring expression was the one he usually got from women these days. Even if it was only The Face she liked, it was better than her earlier reaction. The change seemed strange. Stranger still was the fact it mattered.

Sunny felt like an idiot, giving Pete her warmest smile, but with twenty-eight years of practice, she knew what to do when life threw her a curve. As long as she had to do a televised date with this guy, she'd make the best of it. All she had to do was act as if Pete were the answer to a single girl's prayer. He was probably used to that role. It was only TV, and she'd played "pretend" all of her life.

As he settled into the love seat beside her, Pete's arm touched hers lightly, briefly. Just one touch, but tingles radiated along her arm. It was all she could do to keep from rubbing the sensation away. Her heart raced, but it had to be from nerves, not awareness.

"Sunny Keegan," she said, extending her hand.

"Pete Maguire," he responded, taking hers. His hand was slightly callused, a working man's hand, and his handshake was confident, firm, just right.

Sitting slightly sideways, he slid his arm along the low-backed cushion behind her. His scent was exactly the way she liked men to smell, faintly of soap and woodsy aftershave, not that he was leaning too close or coming on to her. Any man Pete's size took a little more than his share of the room.

He seemed almost shy, but that only proved he was an even better actor than she was, for certainly he knew what those bad-boy eyes did to a woman. Who could ignore eyes like that? The way they crinkled at the corners when he smiled, they could steal her heart away and make her glad they had. Heaven help her if she let herself fall for another handsome charmer.

A bubbly, balding man introduced himself as the date coordinator. "You guys!" he exclaimed, beaming at them. "You're something else. Looks like your date will have to be a two-parter."

"Two-parter?" Pete echoed, sounding startled. "You mean go out twice?" Disbelief filled those blue eyes.

Sunny didn't know what he was so upset about. A guy with Pete's looks didn't come on a show like *Dream Date* because he needed a date. He probably wanted to get noticed by someone in show business. You'd think he'd be happy with more TV exposure.

"Most of the time we send our couples to a restaurant or a resort for their dream date," mused the coordinator, "but it will take a couple of dates to reflect your preferences. There's the backpacking, the camping…"

"We can skip that part," Pete muttered.

"The home cooking…"

"A restaurant's good," Sunny said. "In fact, I'd love a restaurant!"

"Well, yes, but we've got to do the home-cooking thing."

"Not for me we don't," Pete said flatly. "I can have pot roast some other time." One corner of his mouth tilted. "With Mom in her backyard."

"Thanks, kids. Nice attitude."

"It's asking a lot for Sunny to cook," Pete persisted.

She agreed. Totally.

"The problem is," the coordinator said with professional patience, "the next time you're on, the audience will expect your date to reflect the matches you made on this show."

"Next time?" Pete murmured.

Sunny heard him, but the coordinator either didn't or ignored the alarm in Pete's voice.

"For the first part of the date, Sunny, we'll have you cook Pete's favorite dinner at your place."

Sunny couldn't hold back a tiny whimper.

"Or at Pete's if you'd rather."

"No!" If she had to provide a meal, she'd take the home court advantage. "My place is fine."

"What was the menu?" the coordinator asked an assistant.

"Pot roast, mashies and corn on the cob."

"Don't forget the cheesecake," Pete muttered bleakly.

"Chocolate chip," she added, trying hard not to laugh. Talk about a stretch. No way could she manage that meal.

The coordinator checked his list. "That's right. We can't forget dessert! Sunny, we'll provide groceries, flowers, candlelight, wine, the works. If you'd like, we'll send in a cleaning team to make everything party perfect."

She should seem appreciative, but it just wasn't in her. They could forget the flowers and keep the cleaners. Send a chef.

Frowning slightly at his notes, the coordinator continued. "For the backpacking/camping part of your…"

A faint sound, maybe a groan, came from Pete's direction. Again, it was so soft, Sunny thought she may have been the only one to hear it, especially when the coordinator went right on talking about Big Bear and free camping gear.

She glanced Pete's way and saw he'd shaded his eyes with his hand. The lower half of his face looked grim. She wasn't thrilled with the plans, either, but she had the decency to hide it.

"Any questions?" the coordinator asked. "No? Then I guess that wraps it up. Have fun, kids. You make a great-looking couple. We'll see you here in the studio in a couple of weeks for the report-back taping. Okay?"

It wasn't, but Sunny had the manners to fake it. Pete, on the other hand, didn't even look up. What was his problem?

As the staff left the room, Pete stirred from his end of the couch. Leaning toward her, he touched her arm. "Are you going to be all right with this?"

Probably not, but he'd never know it. "Sure," she answered, flashing him her biggest smile. "Just get me the recipe for your mom's cheesecake."

# Chapter Two

Sunny lay on her cream leather sofa, uncomfortable in a pair of too-tight jeans and a skimpy sweater, while the team finished her "home-cooked" meal. One of the mothers had made Pete's cheesecake, and another had taken care of the rest. The girls had arranged everything, right down to setting the table with her grandmother's china. They were such good kids. Working with them this past year had been the happiest time of her life.

Mouse, the team's point guard, bent over her and used a pick to lift sections of Sunny's hair, squirting spray as she went.

"Mouse, don't you think that's enough?" Sunny didn't want to hurt the girl's feelings, but already her hair was a wild, sexy mane with a life of its own.

"It's gotta be perfect, Coach. Once everybody sees this on TV, your ex won't bother you anymore and the talk 'round school will shut down. Everybody's gonna know he's a liar.''

That was youth speaking. Sunny knew people could say and print almost anything, and others would believe it. Her skin was thick, but the girls were still idealistic enough to expect fairness. It bothered them that people believed Bruce and were describing her as coldhearted, self-centered and worse.

She didn't like the idea of the kids being involved with her problems, but getting them to leave her alone was like getting a fast-breaking team to stall.

Leteisha, the team's six-foot center, hovered above her. "Coach, are you concentrating on your date?"

"Not really," she answered honestly.

"There's nothing more important than your date, Coach. You gotta focus."

Words from her own mouth.

"That's right," Mouse said, her dark eyes shining. "You are supposed to think about this hot guy. He is, like, very sexy, and you want him madly."

"Easy, Mouse," Leteisha warned.

"But I think Coach ought to…"

"Not now, girl!"

Sunny hid a smile. Leteisha ran the team with a firm hand.

"Okay, Coach," Leteisha said, her dark eyes sincerely determined. "Let's go over what you're supposed to do. Have you got your plays straight?"

Obediently Sunny recited, "Take the pot roast and mashed-potato casserole out of the oven. Nuke the corn. The gravy's on the range. Salad and cheesecake in the refrigerator. Okay?''

''You forgot the apron.''

She wished they had.

''You need it, Coach, for realism.''

''And to protect your outfit,'' added Mouse, who'd chosen the miniskirt for the TV show and the tight jeans and sweater tonight.

Sunny disliked the sweater as much as she had the miniskirt. The sweater was white—never her color, though with the amount of makeup they had on her, it probably wouldn't matter—and it clung like a second skin. Surely Mouse would take pity on her if she complained once more.

''This sweater is so tight, I can't breathe. Please, Mouse, choose something else.''

''No, no! You must wear it! My brother says a man cannot resist a woman in a tight, white top.''

''Ooooo,'' the girls crooned.

Sunny lifted a brow at them, but it didn't have its usual sobering effect. In fact, one of them, probably Heather, couldn't suppress a giggle.

Circling Sunny as an artist would study her masterpiece, Mouse said, ''Coach, you've got to help that sweater. Use better posture. Throw your shoulders back, and...''

''I've got the idea, Mouse.''

So did the team. They hooted, loving every moment despite her embarrassment.

''All right, you guys,'' Leteisha ordered, pulling Sunny to her feet. ''Huddle up.''

The girls swarmed Sunny as they did during a time-out. Leteisha held up her hand, and a hush fell.

"Okay, Coach, after this date Mr. Big Deal Bruce Daniels is going to know for sure he's been 'ex-ed.'"

"He's history," somebody said.

"For-got-ten!" said another.

"That's right," Leteisha confirmed, shushing further comments with a look. "Now, we've got you this far, but, Coach, you've got to do your part."

"We're counting on you, Coach," Mouse said. "When the TV camera's on you, you gotta make the date look real good."

"'Real good?'" she repeated, not at all sure she'd want to comply with their standards.

"Just be all over the guy, Coach."

"Yeah, make him sweat."

"Put a liplock on him."

"Practice safe—"

"Enough!" Sunny shouted. She loved these kids, but they got out of hand so quickly.

"Settle down," Leteisha bellowed. "You know how Coach feels about that kind of talk. How's she gonna go on national TV with all this hassle? We're here to give her our support."

The girls quieted down but grinned, unrepentant.

Mouse waved an emerald-green chef's apron and sung out, "Coach needs to put this on."

"Thanks, Mouse. Let's get that apron on you, Coach."

Sunny groaned.

"See how nice it goes with your hair?" Mouse coaxed, slipping the apron over Sunny's hair.

At least it would cover the tight, white sweater.

"Go over the game plan, Mouse," Leteisha ordered.

"Okay. Coach, after you answer the door, pretend you forgot to take the apron off and act real embarrassed."

She probably would be.

"Then take your time untying the strings."

"Take a lot of time," Leteisha added with a wicked smile.

"Slip the apron off slow," Mouse coached.

"Yeah, reeeeeeal slow."

"Yeah, like you're doin' a striptease."

"Then the guy sees you in that tight, white top and…"

"It blows his mind!"

The girls high-fived and yelled like they'd just scored the winning basket on a shot from midcourt.

"That does it!" Sunny ordered. "You're out of here!"

Proud of themselves, the team called out outrageous advice all the way to their cars.

Girls! You took two steps forward with them and one step back. She'd never been as bold, but then Eleanor Keegan's daughter had known her manners before she'd known her ABC's.

They were good kids, and they'd worked hard all season, playing with more heart than ability. She'd felt safe promising them anything if they'd win the championship. Of course, now that she knew kids could play over their heads, she'd be careful giving out blank checks.

Winning a championship had been an unexpected thrill and confirmation she was making her life count. Things would be great once she convinced her family to leave her alone. For the girls and herself, she would get through this evening and do her best to dazzle Pete Maguire…if she didn't break out in hives.

Her burst of confidence lasted until the doorbell rang. "Take deep breaths," she told herself. "Lots of deep breaths. Focus. Be convincing. Pretend you're happy to see this guy."

Donning a welcoming smile, she opened the door in a swoop and struck a pose.

But Meggy, the woman from *Dream Date,* stood there.

So much for dazzling.

"Hi, Sunny," the woman said brightly. "We're set up and ready for Pete to arrive. Everything okay here?"

She nodded, forcing her plastic public smile.

"Good. Like we said on the phone, try to ignore the cameras. We'll shoot some stuff to establish Part One of your date and be gone before you know it."

"Great. That's just great. Really great."

*Pull yourself together, Sunny. Use that college education. Speak in multisyllables.* "Are we on schedule?"

"Yes, we are. In fact, Pete ought to arrive in just a few minutes. Have fun."

"Thanks." Sunny closed the door and worked on the breathing exercises she'd taught the girls for pregame jitters. From now on, she'd have a new respect for people who went before the cameras for a living.

She wondered if Pete was as nervous about all

this as she was. Probably not. Not with his experience charming the ladies.

Pete popped a fourth antacid into his mouth and wished he'd been an only child. It was plenty nerve-wracking sitting here in the rental new-model pickup Meggy had paid for so he wouldn't look like a pauper on national TV.

A pauper. He could buy a fleet of new pickups if he wanted to. It was his business what he drove, and he liked driving Old Red, no matter how much money he had. Things like loyalty were important, and he'd had Old Red since high school.

The *Dream Date* staffer who'd stopped him a block from Sunny's place handed Pete a two-way radio. Meggy's voice came through. "Pete, how are you doing?"

"How do you think? Let's get this over with."

"Uh, Pete, the audience always loves it when the guy brings the girl a flower. Teresa's got one there for you."

The staffer handed Pete a red rose.

"What next, Meggy? A stuffed animal?"

"No, we didn't think Coach Keegan seemed like the stuffed animal type. But it would be nice if you'd give her a hug."

"It would be nice if you'd ease up."

"Sorry, Pete, the staff and I—" she paused, letting it sink in that others were listening "—don't mean to be pushy. We're here to make your date successful."

For the benefit of those others, he gushed. "You've done a super job, Meggy. I mean it. If I sounded…unappreciative, it's because all this is pretty strange to me.''

"We understand. No problem. When you're ready, drive on down to the house. Try not to look at the cameras.''

Nervous as a kid up to bat at his first big game, Pete approached Sunny's condo, where a TV van and dozens, maybe hundreds, of teenagers surrounded the place.

*Lord, if you're out there and listening, get me through this. I'd take it as a personal favor if You'd see to it that my hip doesn't act up and I don't make a fool of myself.*

When he stepped out of the pickup, his eyes swept the scene to get his bearings. Naturally he looked right into a camera. Sorry, Meggy.

Fixing his eyes on Sunny's door, he made his way there. Concentrating as hard as he was, he forgot the rose clutched in his hand until he knocked on the door, and the thing jiggled in his grip. When the door swung open, his hand held the rose in midair, raised in a salute. He felt like a fool.

But Sunny's smile was so beautiful and warm, it didn't seem to matter. Those soft butternut eyes affected him the same way they had on the show. He felt the same zing in his gut. The same shortness of breath.

She glanced at the rose in his hand, and he remembered his manners, offering it to her.

"Thank you," she said sweetly, touching her nose to the flower, sniffing its fragrance. "What a nice thing to do.''

He thought about giving Meggy the credit, but

noticed from the corner of his eye that the camera was recording the whole thing. This was as bad as being on the show.

What else had Meggy said he should do? Oh, yeah, the hug. Well, he wasn't giving hugs because his sister said to; however, Sunny looked as if she could use one. Unless he'd lost the ability to read a woman's eyes, she was plenty shaken by this.

As she stepped aside and motioned for him to come in, Pete slid his arm around her waist tentatively. He didn't want her to get the idea that he was a lech or anything, but a friendly "we're in this thing together" kind of hug should be okay.

As if the hug were her own idea, Sunny snuggled into it, and Pete felt his heartbeat pick up. Except for Meggy and his mom, it had been a long time since he'd been this close to a woman. It was ridiculous how much he liked it.

She lifted her face and there wasn't a thing he could do but give her a kiss—just a friendly "glad to see you" kiss. That's what he intended. Who knew it would ignite into a genuine, man-to-woman, take-his-breath-away kiss? Panic ripped through his brain before instinct took over, and he deepened the kiss.

"Get a bucket of water," someone said, "or hose 'em down."

The rude interruption pulled them apart. Pete's heart pounded as if he'd jogged for miles. Sunny's face and neck were flushed, and those big, golden brown eyes looked flustered.

Her embarrassment was his fault. On second thought, the loudmouth had a lot to answer for. Pete turned, ready to silence the man, but Meggy beat him to it.

"Shut up, Brad," she said to her camera operator.

"But we've got enough of this shot. They can do that on their own time. I don't want to be here all night."

"Shut up, or give me the camera and go to the van. We can do this without you."

The guy clamped his jaw, and Pete grinned. Watching his sister back the guy down was sweeter than doing it himself.

"Score one for Meggy," Sunny whispered as she pulled him inside. "I'm ready to join her fan club."

That made two of them.

Sunny had set a table for two in a bay window. Classy, he thought. Real classy. He didn't know they made glasses with stems that tall. "You've gone to a lot of trouble," he said.

"Actually I haven't," she said, an honest-to-goodness blush on her cheeks.

Pete liked modesty in a woman. "Everything looks great, and the food smells good, too."

"Thanks. Dinner's ready. Shall we eat now?"

"Why don't we get our guests out of here first?" Turning toward the door as the crew struggled in with their equipment, he said, "Meggy, I believe you said this wouldn't take long?"

"It won't. All we need is a few seconds of this and that to establish Part One of your date. Let's start with a shot in the kitchen."

Sunny led the way into a large, light-filled room filled with sleek cupboards, expensive-looking appliances and lush plants. Pete had worked on units like this. They didn't come cheap. Teachers' pay must be better than he thought.

Sunny was taller than he'd remembered, about five foot eight or nine, tall enough to be a presence in a girls' basketball game, though her slender build belonged to a model. Her gorgeous legs were covered by jeans, but there was no way a guy could complain about the way she looked in those jeans.

Meggy removed the lid from a pot and said, "Umm, gravy. Pete, would you mind standing here while Sunny stirs this?"

Not any more than he minded everything else.

"Sunny, taste the gravy, reach for the salt and shake a little into the pot."

For a woman who liked cooking for her dates, Pete thought Sunny seemed rather ill at ease following Meggy's orders. Of course, a person was probably awkward doing commonplace things in front of cameras.

"Good," Meggy said. "Now, remove whatever's in the oven."

Pete edged Sunny aside and said, "Let me." He looked around for an oven mitt or pot holders, but didn't see any. "Where are your pot holders?"

She looked at him blankly. "Pot holders?"

This TV thing must really be hard on her. "Or an oven mitt?" he suggested.

Sunny felt heat crawl up her neck. She didn't know what he was talking about, but she knew she ought to.

"That's okay," he said, smiling as he reached behind her. "I'll use this." He grabbed a towel off the counter and used it to protect his hands as he lifted the hot pan from the oven.

Ah, that's what he meant. He must think she was a real idiot. A person who supposedly "loved to cook" ought to have a working knowledge of basic kitchen equipment.

How was she going to get through this charade? She still felt unsettled at the way she'd greeted Pete, kissing him as if he'd just come home from a war. Though she'd offered the kiss for the folks in TV land, she'd felt its impact down to her toes. And Pete? He'd reacted as if it *were* his homecoming.

"Did you get the shot of Pete taking the pan out of the oven, Brad?" Meggy asked.

"Got it. You're gonna love the shot of his backside."

This guy's survival instincts were pretty weak. From the set of Pete's jaw, Sunny would say Brad was asking for trouble.

"We're almost through," Meggy said grimly, apparently fed up with the guy herself. "Let's get a shot of you two at the table, toasting each other."

Toasting she knew how to do, and Sunny breathed easier. From the refrigerator she pulled out a bottle of sparkling cider and handed it to Pete. "Will you do the honors?"

The label seemed to surprise him. She wouldn't argue about it and he didn't have to drink it, but that's all she kept in the house. "Nonalcoholic," she said with no apology.

"Good," he said, going to work unwrapping the seal.

That was different. Her ex always ridiculed her beverage preference.

Muscles rippled in Pete's arm as he opened the bottle, and the fabric of his blue denim shirt strained across his broad, muscular back. This was a guy who worked out.

There was a tiny scar intersecting his left eyebrow that she hadn't noticed before, and faint scars near his ear and under his chin. Strangely, the imperfections made her more comfortable.

"Do you want to get the glasses?" he asked.

"What? Oh, sure." Sunny retrieved them from the table, wondering why he hadn't taken the bottle there. Maybe he wanted more time away from Brad and his camera. That she understood.

He took one goblet and filled it. "I thought we could use a minute without an audience," he said, confirming her suspicion. "Your dinner looks great."

"I just hope it's half as good as your mother's," she said, knowing it wouldn't be if she'd cooked it.

"I expect it's even better."

He smiled again, and Sunny's heart seemed to contract. The shine in those blue eyes made her wonder if all handsome charmers had to be bad.

They carried their glasses to the dining area, and Meggy asked, "Sunny, do you want to keep the apron on?"

Oops. She'd forgotten the thing, maybe subconsciously, for as much as she had resisted wearing the apron, she now dreaded taking it off. She knew she had a good figure, but she took pride in the condition of her body, its strength and health, not its shape, and she never purposely called attention to herself. However, she'd better follow orders unless she wanted to hear about it from Mouse.

Untying the apron was a bit tedious because somehow she'd knotted the strings. Getting the apron over her head without messing up her big hair was slow-going, too. Finally she tossed the apron aside and sneaked a glance at Pete to see if Mouse's brother was right about the tight white top.

He was. Appreciation registered in Pete's eyes.

"N-i-c-e sweater!" Brad said with a low whistle.

Pete's head whipped around, and he took a threatening step toward the man, but Meggy said, "Brad, for the last time, if you want to work for *Dream Date* again, keep quiet."

"You're the boss," he said irreverently. "What do you want to do about the glare from the window by the table?"

"Should I pull the shade?" Sunny asked.

"No. It'll make a tighter shot if you sit beside, instead of across from Pete." Meggy maneuvered them into position, changing the place settings as she talked.

"Sunny, hold your goblet in your right hand, rest your elbow on the table and lean toward Pete. Pete, hold—"

"I got it, Meggy," he interrupted.

"It'll be over soon," Sunny whispered.

His rueful smile was endearing. "Sorry about the attitude."

"Don't worry about it. I understand."

"We're rolling," Meggy said. "Touch glasses, take a sip, do what comes naturally."

Pete touched the rim of his goblet to Sunny's and whispered, "Punching Brad's face in comes naturally."

"Let me be the one to do it," she whispered back.

He grinned and toasted her again.

Her heart did its strange flip-flop just like before.

"Did I see antipasto on the table, Sunny?" Meggy asked.

"Yes. Shall we eat some?"

"You might feed each other a bite or two."

"I don't usually finger feed on a first date," she said, a nervous giggle escaping. Mortified, she covered her mouth, struggling for control.

Pete looked longingly at the door. What if he balked here and now? As long as she'd endured the torture of the TV taping, she'd like to see this through.

Sobering, she said, "You go first. I like those big black olives. Do you want to pop one of them into my mouth?"

He followed her directions to the letter, popping the olive into her mouth with all the aplomb of a guy feeding a heartworm pill to his dog.

"C'mon, Pete," Meggy complained, "you can do better than that. You're on a date. Make it look sensual."

Pete raised an irritated brow. "What do you think?" he murmured. "Should we try it her way?"

"I like black olives so much, I can probably make it 'look sensual.'"

"Okay, one sensual olive coming your way," he warned, leaning toward her, teasing her mouth with the olive, outlining her upper lip and tracing the lower lip back and forth before slipping it between her teeth. She bit down slowly, covering his fingers with her lips. Slowly he dragged his fingers away. She had no idea that such a simple thing could be so erotic.

"Whew," he breathed softly, watching her lips as she slowly chewed. "I like the way you do that."

"Really," she murmured. "It didn't look stupid?"

"Are you kidding?" His eyes glowed with approval.

The approval caught her by surprise. It felt warm, wonderful and better than she could have believed.

It would have to be better still without an audience. She whispered, "Don't you think we've been cooperative long enough?"

Nodding, he stood and said, "You're through here, aren't you, Meggy?"

Something unspoken passed between the two. Sunny didn't understand it, but Meggy quickly agreed and managed to get the crew out within minutes. Whatever it was, it didn't matter. It was just good to have their audience gone.

Standing next to Pete in the doorway, seeing them off, Sunny felt awkward, almost shy. It was ridiculous, feeling this nervous about being alone with a guy. She was twenty-eight, not sixteen, and it sure didn't matter if he invited her to the prom.

Pete closed the door and gave her one of those lopsided smiles. "Coach, you were awesome. Poised. Cute. A dream date, for sure."

It was a line. It had to be, but she didn't feel nervous anymore. "You were pretty great yourself," she said, wanting to return the good feeling. "An old pro, in fact."

"That's me, all right. An old pro. I can't wait to see myself on TV."

The sarcasm surprised her. She must have shown it.

He added, "Well, it's not like I'm the most photogenic guy in town. I always look awkward in home movies."

*Awkward* was not a word she would have used to describe Pete Maguire, not in a million years. "You've got to be joking. You couldn't look bad if you tried."

He looked at her as if she'd lost her mind.

"Well, you couldn't," she insisted.

As quickly as a cloud steals the sun, Pete's blue eyes dulled. The sadness, the loss in those eyes took her breath away. What was wrong? Was it something she said?

Pete felt like a fool. It wasn't the first time he'd forgotten the new cheekbones, Roman nose and classic chin. When he looked in a mirror these days, it wasn't him. Sometimes he felt like an alien the way people treated The Face as if it were real. The few times he tried to explain, he got pity or skepticism. Even worse was the advice he should be grateful.

Why didn't people understand he wasn't somebody brand-new just because he looked it? Whoever said what counted was the person inside had never had reconstructive facial surgery. People wouldn't let you be the person inside. They reacted to what they saw. Or thought they saw.

It was better to live like a hermit, hang out at the beach by himself and get through the days, one at a time, until he got comfortable with all the changes. If he ever did.

He should never have let Meggy talk him into this date.

Determined to escape, but not wanting to hurt Sunny's feelings—she was too nice a person for that—he said, "Now that the cameras are gone, I should probably head out, too."

"Head out?" she echoed, her pretty brown eyes perplexed. "You want to leave now? Was it something I said?"

"No!" He didn't want her to think that. "It's just…I think I should go. I'm not very good company."

She shrugged. "You're a lot better than Brad."

He liked her quick comeback even if she wasn't letting him bow out gracefully. "I may be better than Brad, but believe me, you can do better than me—a whole lot better."

"The audience didn't seem to think so. What am I supposed to do with all this food?" she asked, her hands on her hips, her stance defiant, as if she were arguing with a ref who'd just called a foul on a good blocked shot. "We've got pot roast, Pete, and mashed potatoes with gravy, corn on the cob and the cheesecake. In fact, everything but your mom and her backyard."

"What would you say if I told you I don't eat red meat, I hate cheesecake, my mom never cooks and she has no backyard."

Surprise flared in those butternut eyes, but she

quipped, "What would you say if I told you I didn't cook a speck of this food and, in fact, can't even boil water?"

He felt the smile break across his face.

"You think that's funny? We'll see who's laughing if you don't eat this food. My girls will track you down and use that ugly tie you wore on *Dream Date* to hang you by your neck."

Maybe he ought to try the pot roast. If Sunny served it, he might even like cheesecake.

# Chapter Three

"Who'd you say cooked the pot roast?" Pete said, sopping gravy with the last of his mashed potatoes.

"Leteisha's mother."

"Lucky Leteisha. Was your mom a good cook?"

"A wonderful woman named Cook did our cooking."

"Hmm. A guy named McDonald did most of ours. I learned to love peanut butter. Now it's a vice."

She laughed and silently thanked Pete for not pursuing her family background.

"So, do you want to invite the team over for cheesecake?" he said, leaning back in his chair, dangling his goblet in one hand.

"You aren't trying to slip out on me again, are you?"

He grinned. "No, I just thought the girls had

worked pretty hard on this meal and deserved a treat.''

"It's more than that. Confess. You want someone to eat your piece of cheesecake.''

He worked that crooked smile and nodded. "Guilty,'' he said, not looking it, not for a minute, not with those teasing eyes.

"We'd better not have the girls over. Mouse would have a fit if she knew I'd changed out of that top.''

"That was a great top.'' The appreciative gleam in his eye made her as self-conscious as she'd been in the sweater.

"I thought I ought to work on that gravy stain right away. The sweater belonged to her.''

"Very considerate.''

He wouldn't think so if he knew she'd spilled the gravy on purpose. She felt bad about it, but she'd buy Mouse a dozen sweaters if need be. She'd just had to get out of that thing.

"The way your girls brought this whole thing off, it's no wonder they won the regional. You must be some coach, Sunny Keegan.''

The words might be pure shmooze, the stock and trade of handsome men, but she didn't mind, not this once. "The girls deserve all the credit,'' she said, trying not to enjoy his praise too much.

"I can't believe the trouble they went to, getting you on *Dream Date* and all.''

"They were dead serious about getting me a date.''

"They thought they had to fix *you* up?" His astonishment was real and very flattering.

It gave her the courage to tell him what he'd probably find out anyhow. He deserved the truth, and she'd rather it came from her. "I hadn't had a date since they'd known me."

His eyes widened in surprise.

She looked away, not wanting to see the inevitable pity her explanation would generate. "Last June I was supposed to be married. Hours before the wedding, I discovered my fiancé with one of my bridesmaids and realized...well, you know."

She risked a glance. It wasn't pity on his face, but anger. That was okay.

"I didn't handle it very well. I knew I couldn't marry him, but I was pretty confused. Maybe it was cowardly, but I just took off and left the explanations to him."

"Cowardly?" His eyebrows rose in protest. "He got off easy. If it were my sister, she'd have shot the guy. What happened when everybody realized you were gone?"

"My dad stood beside Bruce at the altar and told everyone the wedding was postponed because I was ill."

"Postponed?"

She nodded.

"And you didn't tell anyone what you saw." He said it as a statement, not a question, as if he understood she'd rather live the lie than have people pity her.

Let people think she was an irresponsible flake. It was better than having them know she was an idiot who'd been taken in. Besides, if her parents hadn't believed her, how could she expect anyone else to?

There was no pity in Pete's eyes, just an awareness of the tough time she'd had. Testing his reaction, she added, "They went ahead and turned the reception into a party, saying I'd insisted on it."

"You've got to be kidding," he said with disgust.

She'd felt the same way, but she had to be fair.

"I ought to explain that my ex and my father are both in politics. It's normal for them to put a spin on a bad situation. That's why they went ahead with the reception."

Pete was obviously baffled. "Let me get this straight. You found your ex messing around, told him it was over and took off. Nobody knew why or where you'd gone, and your parents went ahead and partied with your ex. That doesn't make sense."

Exactly. "Well, that's what happened. My parents believed Bruce, not me. They thought I'd done him a great wrong, jumping to conclusions they way I did. My anger shouldn't have been with Bruce, but with the deranged groupie who'd cornered the poor man and forced herself on him."

"Groupie? Sunny, who is your ex?"

"Congressman Bruce Daniels."

"No way! I voted for the guy!"

"You don't need to again."

"I won't!" Shaking his head in wonder, he murmured, "Politics!"

She smiled. It was rather nice having someone understand, though it still hurt how her parents reacted that night.

"What happened when you confronted Bruce about his lies?" he asked tersely, as if he already knew he wouldn't like the answer.

She grimaced, waving the question away. She didn't care to relive that scene. If Pete understood at all, he'd give her a break on this.

And he did, just muttering under his breath, "Daniels! What a jerk!"

She was human enough to appreciate his distaste and support. It made her feel less alone somehow.

"The gifts were returned," she said, clearing the lump in her throat when the words came out thick with emotion, "but my parents and Bruce still talk about our engagement as if it's an ongoing thing."

"And you don't mind?" Pete asked, incredulous.

"Mind! Of course, I do, but keeping silent has been better than having the facts brought out. They've left me alone until recently. Not long ago Bruce visited a government class at my school and told everyone I was his fiancée. My girls knew I couldn't be engaged to anyone without them knowing it, and they were furious."

"Good for them!"

"Then a tabloid printed a news story that really got the rumor mill spinning. I'm from a political family, so my hide is tough. But the girls can't stand it that I'm seen as heartless and insensitive while Bruce is the long-suffering lover."

"I'm with the girls." He stood abruptly as if he couldn't sit still another minute. "I don't like to see Daniels get away with this."

His righteous anger made her smile. It was great having a champion. "The girls are determined to shut Bruce down. That's why they got me on the show. Don't you think a big-haired babe in pursuit of her dream date ought to give Bruce and my parents a reality check?''

He threw back his head and laughed heartily. It was remarkable what this man did for her morale. She'd even stopped minding that he was way too good-looking.

"Now that I think about it," he said, still chuckling, "that kiss you gave me at the door... That was probably more for the congressman than it was for me." His adorable lopsided smile dared her to deny it.

She shrugged innocently. "Just following orders. The girls said to make it look 'real good.'"

"I expect it did!"

She was lucky he was such a good sport. "If I got a little overenthusiastic, I'm sorry."

"Nothing to be sorry about," he assured her.

"I was really nervous." It was a relief to admit it.

"Really? It was a great kiss. Perfect, in fact."

This guy said all the right things. "You did okay yourself," she said, wanting to return the good feeling.

"Yeah?" His grin turned shy. "I'm a little out of practice."

"Out of practice!" It was her turn to laugh. "You? Pete Maguire? The man Cheryl wanted to go 'exploring' with?"

"I couldn't believe she said that."

"Well, you are pretty cute."

"Cute?"

"Okay, good-looking."

"Let's change the subject."

He was embarrassed. Her ex wouldn't have been. He'd have relished the compliment and fished for more. "If you want to change the subject," she said, "you'll have to do it."

"Fine. I will."

Watching him search for a topic, she smiled, delighted to know there lived a charmer who wasn't totally self-centered.

"This date we're doing," he said thoughtfully, "it won't be on TV for a while. Right?"

"They said in about six weeks."

"That's quite a while. What are you going to do about the rumor mill until then?"

"Things should be better at school after tonight. There were a lot of kids here."

"But what about Daniels? Six weeks is a long time."

"I know. I guess I'll just try not to worry about it."

"Good luck."

"Thanks. I'll need it. But I really will try. Worry tells God I don't trust Him, and I do."

Something crossed his eyes that could have been cynicism, perhaps unbelief. She never argued religion, but the Lord had taken care of her so well, she'd never be ashamed of Him. "The Bible says God will 'devour any who would rise up against me.' I believe it."

Pete's eyes narrowed, and she thought he was going to dispute the point. But he leaned forward, touched her hand and said, "You're one hundred percent right."

"I am?" She couldn't help sounding surprised. "A second ago, I didn't think we were on the same wavelength."

"It took me a second to switch gears. It's been a while since someone's quoted scripture to me. You know, I used to help out with our youth group."

A deep gladness filled her heart. "I'm so happy you know the Lord!"

She'd barely said the words when she wished she could take them back. Such a mix of emotion passed across Pete's face that she couldn't begin to read them all, but she recognized anger and resentment. How could she not, when she'd known them herself?

Pete rose from the table and carried their plates into the kitchen.

Silently she asked God what to do, what to say. She glanced over to her Bible on the coffee table, wondering which scripture she could read that would help Pete the most. Maybe something in John.

But Pete strolled back into the room, and she canceled the Bible study. His lady-killer smile was back, firmly in place, and his eyes glowed with mischief.

"Sunny, how would you like to shut Daniels down right away?"

This guy could really switch gears. "Well, I'd love it."

"What if the media were here when I pick you up for Part Two of our date? Let them get photographs of you greeting me at the door the same way you did tonight. How about that?''

Pete truly was an ally if he could offer to help her, but how could she talk about trusting God one moment and, in the next, take matters into her own hands even more than she already had?

''Pete, I appreciate the offer, but you don't have to do this for me. God really will protect me.''

Those bad-boy eyes lifted innocently. ''You don't think God uses people to carry out his plans? For all you know, I could be an angel in disguise.''

She laughed at the thought. Would God send her a handsome charmer, especially when He knew how much she didn't trust them? Actually, He might, though Pete's feet seemed planted pretty firmly on the ground.

''Are you sure about this?'' she asked, hardly believing this particular guy would set himself up as a media target. He didn't know what it could be like.

''Oh, I think I can make myself kiss a pretty girl when it's for such a good cause. Besides, it's part of the job. As far as angel assignments go, I got lucky. If it hadn't been you, I might have been assigned to Brad.''

She smiled and the good feeling went all the way to her toes. He could be an angel, the way he made her feel that her problems were only tiny white specks on a big, fluffy cloud and contentment was fingertip near.

But he looked nothing like any storybook angel she'd ever seen, not with that lock of black hair falling over his brow, the wicked half smile and the teasing gleam in his eyes. If Pete really were her angel...that was some disguise.

Pete parked his truck in Sunny's drive and sucked in a deep breath. It was the sequel to the circus of the first part of their date, only worse. This time there were several media vehicles, not just the *Dream Date* van, and a couple of squad cars with rotating lights that added to the general confusion. And there was a really big crowd.

His mother always said he was a born protector, but this time he may have overdone it.

Sunny sat on her steps, probably waiting for her cue. Purple bougainvillea cascaded down the side of her condo, a brilliant backdrop for her lush coppery hair. She was a beautiful woman all right.

She'd warned him she was going to take her girls' advice and pretend she was "wild about him." He wasn't sure what that entailed, but whatever it was, he could handle it. It was past time somebody helped Sunny get Bruce Daniels out of her life.

Wearing a headset, looking in charge of things, Meggy walked up to his truck. "How're you doing, bro?"

"Just peachy," he said, trying to hide his nervousness. "Can we get on with this?"

"We're ready and rolling. Go for it."

Determined to silence Sunny's ex-fiancé once and for all, Pete put a big smile on his kisser, got out of the truck and walked up the driveway with his arms spread wide.

Sunny leapt to her feet, ran to meet him and, just as they'd planned, bussed him smack on the mouth.

He returned the kiss, dragging it out, giving it all he had. It was only for show, but it made his heart pound as hard as if it were real. Her lips were soft and giving. She held on to him as if she'd never let go.

"Wow!" he heard Meggy murmur. It must look real if Meggy was impressed.

Even though he knew Sunny was only pretending, he liked the feel of her hands around his neck. Taking her face between his hands, he rained kisses over her brow, her cheeks, her eyes, and ended with one on her mouth that he deepened. He pulled her to him, and the sweet burn was more than he'd expected.

It was all an act, he kept telling himself. But when he broke the kiss, he leaned his forehead against hers, breathing hard.

"Whew," Sunny whispered. "That was great."

Her sweet praise deserved another soft kiss. Just one, but she yielded her mouth so sweetly he forgot how to count.

"Pete?"

"Hmm?"

"You can really kiss."

She made him feel like he'd done something great. "I guess it's like riding a bike," he joked, pulling away. "You never forget even if you're out of practice."

Sunny knew her ex had practiced more than most, but he had never kissed her like that. One more of Pete's kisses and she would melt where she stood.

"That dazed expression on your face is perfect," he said. "I think that's the look you're going for."

That was fortunate. Dazed was all she could manage. "Do you think we're overdoing this?" she muttered, daring a peek at the enthusiastic crowd.

"I don't think so. Act like I'm talking sexy to you," he murmured, placing a gentle kiss on her forehead.

It felt as if he were.

"Where's your gear?"

"At your feet, I think." Funny how a person could lose her bearings on her own driveway.

They parted, and he hoisted her pack.

"Looks like it's seen some wear. *Dream Date* didn't supply you with new?"

"They offered, but I preferred to bring my own."

He took her hand and gave it an encouraging squeeze. "Don't forget to look wild about me."

That would be easy. With his dark hair gleaming in the early-morning sunlight, with those eyes and that smile, who could forget? What woman wouldn't appreciate Pete?

Certainly the crowd of teenage girls did, judging from their noisy approval. She waved to them as he slung her gear in the truck, opened his door and stood aside for her to climb in.

"Nice truck," she said, sliding to the middle of the seat.

He raised an eyebrow at the way she'd left him barely enough room. "This must not be your first date in a pickup."

"As a matter of fact, it is, but I've observed. Unless they're married, the girl sits by the guy in a pickup."

"All the better to cuddle up to her guy," he agreed, climbing in beside her.

Sunny draped her arm around his neck. "How's this?"

"Nice move."

She looked into his eyes with what she hoped was a dreamy expression. "Now, I'm going to ask you something very personal."

He tipped her chin up with one finger. "How personal?"

"Very." She loved the smell of his woodsy aftershave.

"Ask away."

"Okay. Let me see. How many miles per gallon?"

His blue eyes crinkled at the corner and his stomach shook with quiet laughter. "I don't know. The pickup's a rental."

"You rented a pickup?" She brushed a lock of soft black hair off his forehead as if she had the right. "A pickup isn't really your choice of 'Transportation on a First Date'?"

"Actually, it is," he said, nuzzling her chin, "but Old Red is kind of shy."

"Your truck has a name?"

"It's a rule. Keep a vehicle over ten years, it gets a name."

"I'll have to remember that."

"You don't have a pickup, do you?" he said, testing his instincts.

"No, that was something else the girls dreamed up for me."

"And your favorite form of transportation is…?"

"I have a Chevy that I drive to school and a Jaguar that was a engagement gift from my parents who thought a champagne convertible was the perfect car for Bruce's wife."

"You don't like it?"

"No, I love it. But it's a little hard to explain on a teacher's salary."

"Still, it was a nice gift."

"They gave Bruce a house."

"No wonder he wants to stay engaged."

He rubbed his nose against hers before kissing the tip. She'd always thought nose-kissing was rather silly, but it wasn't bad, not the way Pete did it. It wasn't easy, keeping this light. Trying, she murmured, "That was a virgin nose you just kissed."

His stomach shook again. "Nobody ever kissed your nose before? How about this hand?"

He took her hand and placed a sweet kiss in the palm. It was such a tender gesture Sunny nearly forgot to breathe.

"Is our audience getting this?"

Sunny stole a look. "There's a cop grinning at us, and my girls are going to hurt themselves, the way they're high-fiving each other. Brad's still got his camera on us."

"Okay, one more big kiss and the show's over."

Gathering her in his arms, pulling her across his chest, Pete kissed her as if he were starving for her. It was only an act, Sunny's mind screamed, but the rest of her just didn't know the difference.

Pulling back, he smoothed her hair. It was such a simple, unexpected gesture, but it stirred something inside. Watching him back out of her drive, she was so glad he'd come into her life.

"You were terrific!" She had to say it, at least this once. "If that doesn't silence Bruce, nothing will."

His slow, sexy smile nearly took her breath away. "Think they'll wonder how we could get so hot and heavy on a first date?"

"Part Two of a first date."

"Right. That explains it." He laughed softly, shaking his head. "I just hope your reputation isn't worse now than it was."

"You're not saying I'm 'easy'?"

"Oh, no, not me. I'm not crazy enough to rile a wild woman when there's no place to run."

"I was pretty wild, wasn't I?"

"No—" he grinned "—you were perfect."

# Chapter Four

Turning in her seat, noticing the TV van had caught up with them, she asked, "How long do you think the *Dream Date* crew will stay with us?"

"Meggy said they would head back once we started up the trail."

"How long should we wait to make sure they're gone before heading back ourselves?" They had agreed they wouldn't actually do Part Two of the date. She didn't feel right about camping overnight with a guy, and Pete said he understood.

"Not long. We could do something else after they're gone," he said, glancing her way to check out her reaction. "Would you like to get something to eat? We don't have to end the date early."

He really did have the sweetest smile she'd ever seen on a guy. It always started in his eyes. She would love to spend more time with him, but he'd already done so much for her, she didn't want to take advantage of his generosity. With studied non-chalance, she said, "Whatever. You decide."

The words were barely out of her mouth when she knew she'd pushed the nonchalance too far. She'd sounded indifferent, as if she could have cared less, and she didn't feel that way at all. They waited through an entire signal light in silence.

"I guess we don't have to decide now," he said quietly.

Dating was the pits. It was for kids who believed in magic and miracles, not for has-beens like herself who knew for a fact that fairy dust fades. She needed to make things right, but she'd never been good with words. She'd majored in physical education, for goodness' sake. She was a person who did it, not said it.

*Lord, help me to know what to say to Pete.*

It was only a little prayer, but it gave her the strength to risk rejection. "How about getting a pizza?" She tried her best smile. "Or a steak? My treat. You choose the place."

He glanced away from the road, checking her out, and a smile slid into place. Giddy, she breathed silent thanks. They'd hurdled the bad spot.

"Let's have pizza," he said decisively, "but I've got to warn you, I'm not a 'one-topping' kind of guy. I like them to run it through the garden, and I'll need a salad, too, so it'll cost you. Think you can spring for all that?"

She'd bet her last nickel Pete would eat nails before he'd let her grab the check, but she was so happy they were comfortable again, that she'd have bought his meals for a week.

"I'll buy the pizza," she said, "if you'll buy dessert."

"Ice cream?"

"Fine, but it's got to be pistachio. I love pistachio. What's your favorite?"

"Vanilla. I'm not much of a risk taker, although there is this place in the valley that sells peanut butter mocha fudge. I like it a lot. Want to try it after the pizza?"

"As long as it's nowhere near San Josita. I don't think I could take being a celebrity there again today."

"No?" He gave her another quick glance. "You were good at it. Even I couldn't tell you were pretending."

It hadn't felt as if she were. "They won't be linking me with Bruce anymore. What shall I say when they ask me about you?"

"Do you think they will?" He seemed astonished at the possibility.

She laughed. "They'll talk all right."

"I guess pretty teachers always get talked about. Now that I think about it, we kept pretty close tabs on our art teacher and the blond teacher who taught French or Spanish. I forget which. They were knockouts. Who did your friends talk about?"

"The dating habits of the nuns at Our Lady of Tears didn't generate much gossip."

"Our Lady of Tears? Never heard of it."

"It's a girls' boarding school near Carmel."

"All girls?" he asked, horrified, or pretending to be. "Did you like that?"

"Did I like what?" She knew what he meant. She'd had this conversation before.

"A school with no guys."

"We saw guys," she said, assuming a lofty air.

He lifted a brow. "With a telescope trained on the beach?"

She smacked his arm. "No! For your information, there was a mountain between us and the beach."

"Bummer. So you girls didn't date?"

"It was a prep school, Maguire. Parents didn't send their daughters there for the social life."

"Prep school, huh? Sounds more like a juvie prison. Were you a bad girl, Sunny Keegan?"

The very idea of Eleanor Keegan's daughter being a bad girl made her laugh aloud. "I'll have you know, there's a waiting list to get into Our Lady of Tears."

"Go figure," he said, shaking his head in wonder. "I wouldn't have liked an all-boys school. Not once those hormones kicked in."

"We had a social life. They arranged events with an all-boys school nearby. Dances, cookouts, mixers, all heavily chaperoned."

"Doesn't sound much different than a Dream Date."

"The dress code was. Cheryl couldn't have gotten away with her low-cut dress, and Kevin couldn't have worn those holey jeans."

"How about my tie? Betcha all the little preppies wore ties."

"Not with grapes on them."

He grinned at her. "You really checked me out, didn't you?"

"Not necessarily. I just couldn't miss that ugly tie."

He laughed silently. "How about little short skirts? Did the nuns let you wear leather?"

"Never!"

"Pity. I liked that skirt. You've got great legs, Coach."

How was she supposed to respond to that? She felt the heat build in her face.

"You want some coffee?" he asked. "There's a thermal jug and cups on the floor."

That was impressive. Bruce might have wanted coffee on an early-morning drive, but he would have expected her to bring it.

"If you need cream and sugar, I threw some packets in the glove compartment."

"Pretty thoughtful."

"No, just habit. Lisa couldn't stand black coffee."

Neither could Sunny until that moment. If it choked her, she'd drink hers plain. Whoever Lisa was, Sunny didn't want to be anything like her. It was irrational, but instinctive, as natural as her sudden desire to know everything about Lisa.

Pete seemed comfortable with the silence between them, and she didn't mind, for it gave her more time to wonder about the mystery woman. He had said, "Lisa couldn't stand black coffee." "Couldn't" was definitely past tense. So Lisa was an ex. Ex what? Girlfriend, wife, coffee drinker? What?

Sunny sipped the bitter black brew and focused on the blossoming ice plants that turned the freeway into a gorgeous pink corridor. It was ridiculous to speculate about some woman in Pete's past, and she wouldn't do it, not at all. She had great discipline.

Channeling that discipline, she wondered how many calories she would save by giving up cream in her coffee. She wondered if spring was Pete's favorite season as it was hers. And she concluded that Lisa had to be a long-term part of Pete's life if he'd developed habits of consideration toward her.

Lisa could be anybody. What earthly difference did it make? It was tacky, giving reign to curiosity. Powerful, consuming, raging curiosity that would not be denied. "Who's Lisa?" she had to ask.

"Lisa?" he repeated, frowning.

"You mentioned her a minute ago."

He looked at her with a blank expression.

"You said Lisa didn't like black coffee," she prompted.

His lip curled. "Black coffee was just one of the things she didn't like. Lisa was my wife. She divorced me two years ago."

It was rude to pry, but polite to show interest. "Were you married long?"

"Ten years, and we went together all through high school."

He'd volunteered that, but it had a bitter ring that reminded her why it was bad to be nosy. She stored her coffee cup, stared blindly out the window and waited for him to share what he wanted. It wasn't worth wasting a beautiful morning, forcing the man to talk.

Pete tapped the steering wheel in a mindless rhythm, annoyed with himself, irritated that he'd let Lisa intrude on the first, well, second, date he'd ever had with someone besides her. Why had he mentioned her? She ought to be so far back in his brain that he couldn't even think of her name, let alone her coffee preferences.

He hated thinking about Lisa and his old life. No good ever came of it. That's why he stuck to his routine, going to the beach every day, going home every night. As long as he followed the pattern, he could get through a whole day without once thinking of himself as a loser.

He had Meggy to thank for yanking him out of his comfortable rut. She thought nothing of invading his privacy, expecting him to bail her out time after time. To be fair, helping her out was his choice. That's the way love worked in their family. But he wished she'd just leave him alone.

Someday, when he was ready, he'd find something more productive to do than being a beach bum. Maybe he'd even find a nice girl, someone like Sunny who was so undemanding and self-sufficient, she'd pray for an angel to come to her aid before she'd expect it from him.

Only, he doubted there was anybody else quite like Sunny, a woman who was pretty from the inside out. He liked being with her and couldn't help wondering what it would have been like if this camping trip were the real thing.

He could imagine them sitting by a campfire in the quiet wilderness, with her snuggled up beside him and him stealing a couple of kisses. Well, actually, probably more than a couple. Her kisses weren't the kind a man rationed. But not too many.

Not so many that things got out of hand. He still thought some things you saved for marriage.

It was a nice fantasy. He didn't know berries about camping, but he could read up or hire somebody to teach him. There were plenty of nice places to camp besides Big Bear where the rough terrain would be more than his hip could take—at least that's what the doctors and therapists said.

Man, he was tired of being told what he could and couldn't do. None of those experts knew how good he felt. He walked three miles a day, worked out and ate healthy. He was strong as an ox and determined. Someday he'd get back to where he had been.

So what if a jury thought it couldn't be done. All they'd had were facts, figures and doctors' reports. None of that measured heart. One of these days the insurance company would check in, see the recovery he'd made and want their millions back.

Since they weren't actually going to do the hike, he hadn't told Sunny about his limitations. He could tell her. He was no macho stud. He admitted weakness, sometimes. The problem was, if he told her, she'd get all sympathetic. He'd seen enough pitying eyes to last him a lifetime.

He sneaked a glance at her. Man, she was pretty, sitting there in her jeans and yellow T-shirt. The front had some kind of Christian graphic on it, but he couldn't make out what it was without staring at her chest.

It was nice, riding along with a pretty girl, feeling like his old self. He should take a page from Sunny's book and stop worrying. God could take care of him, that is, if God wanted to.

Sunny drained the last of her nasty, black coffee and wondered if drinking it this way was worth keeping Pete's mind off Lisa. He hadn't said if they'd had children, but he seemed the kind of man who would talk about them, even show pictures, if he had any. He would make a terrific father. She knew that, though she was no expert on fathers. Or mothers. But if she ever had a baby, her child would never doubt how much he was loved, and he'd always be able to trust his mom.

When had she stopped trusting her parents? It was long before the wedding fiasco. Resentment was an old, old emotion, one that she loaned to the Lord when she ought to give it to Him for keeps.

Sometimes, when she went before the Lord, it got in the way. The Word was clear on the subject. She couldn't have unloving feelings toward anyone and also say she loved God.

*Lord, forgive me for dwelling on the past again. It's a human thing to do, but it brings no glory to your Son. Once more, help me realize I've never walked this way before. It's a new day, and You have a plan for me. You're here, and I trust You.*

It was true. The Holy Spirit was here and His sweet sense of peace. No wonder the Word said to "pray always" and to "continue in prayer." She took a deep, cleansing, satisfying breath and let it out slowly, relishing His comfort.

"I believe that sounded like a sigh of contentment," Pete said, smiling, his eyes crinkling at the corners the way she liked.

"I was thanking God for this beautiful day."

He glanced at her warily. It didn't matter. She'd gotten used to that look ever since she'd started talking openly about God. Her beloved nanny had taught her to keep religion private out of consideration for others, but these days God was so real, she had to acknowledge Him. How could it hurt, as long as she didn't judge?

"I love being in the mountains," she said conversationally so Pete wouldn't be uncomfortable. "Where do you usually hike?"

He checked his mirrors, the rearview and sides, before answering. "No one place."

Her hooey detector buzzed an alarm. He wasn't being quite honest. Or maybe he thought it was none of her business.

"From the look of your gear, you must be a serious backpacker," he said, inviting hiking conversation.

She relaxed, chiding her suspicious mind. She'd been around teenagers too long, suspecting things that weren't there. "I love hiking, but it's a new interest. After I broke off with Bruce, I found I liked getting away from everybody and everything."

Pete understood perfectly. He'd become a loner when his life fell apart.

"There's something so peaceful about being in the wilderness with the vastness of God's creation all around," she said dreamily.

"For me, it's the ocean. I love the sound, the sight, the reassuring sameness of the tide."

"An endless reminder of God's power."

He'd never been with someone so at ease talking

about God. He agreed with what she'd said, but it wouldn't have occurred to him to say it.

"The thing I like about hiking," she mused, "is you can't dwell on the everyday stuff. You're caught up in your surroundings, and pretty soon everything's right with the world."

"I think you might have enjoyed Part Two of our date," he said ruefully.

She gave him that big, beautiful smile. "I am enjoying it. Much more than I thought I would! Remind me to tell you my first impression when we have more time. This is our turnoff, and I need a minute to get back into character. I want to be wild about my man!"

His heart beat picked up, and his grin felt so wide, he probably looked goofy. "Anything I can do to help?"

She released her seat belt and scooched over beside him. "Just drive carefully. I'm going beltless."

The way she crowded beside him and put her head on his shoulder was enough to make a man hit the brakes and really drag out the trip.

"Nice move, Coach. You've done this before."

She giggled. "Nuh-uh. It just seems to come naturally."

He lifted his arm, tucked it around her and drove with one hand. Should they get ticketed for the belt infraction, he wouldn't care if they doubled the fine. He felt like a young dude, riding the strip on a Friday night with the prettiest girl in town.

"Are Meggy and the crew still behind us?" she asked.

''We lost Meggy when we turned off the freeway, but I'm sure she'll show up.''

Since she'd been about three, his sister could track him down better than a dog could find his way back home. Her radar never failed, no matter what he did to throw her off the scent. It was sheer luck she hadn't discovered his present hideout.

He parked the truck, and Sunny asked, ''How do you want to divide up the gear?''

Divide up the gear? He hadn't looked through the equipment *Dream Date* sent. Lisa had always nagged him about stuff like that. He didn't mind flying by the seat of his pants, but women weren't happy unless they were a tad overorganized.

''Why don't we just carry our own?''

''But if any real hikers watch the show, they wouldn't expect us to go off with packs bigger than an overnight requires. Neither would they expect us to carry duplicate gear. You know how it is. At the end of the day, four extra pounds feels like forty.''

''Okay, we'll just use one pack, and I'll carry it.''

She looked incredulous. ''Nobody does that! Women carry their share of the load, Pete.''

Man, hiking protocol was as big a deal as golf etiquette.

''However, they would expect us to share a tent. Do you want to use yours or mine? Mine will sleep two. It's pretty small, but long enough for tall people like us to stretch out in.''

''Why not pack real light and forget the tent? There's always the Starlight Hotel.''

''Cute, Pete. I don't know where you hike, but on Big Bear the weather's so changeable you never know what to expect. The last time I was here it rained during the night. The time before, it snowed.''

He was definitely in over his head. From now on, he'd keep his mouth shut and go along with anything she suggested.

''Just kidding,'' he said, trying to sound as if he were.

''Your stove or mine?'' Sunny asked, digging into her gear.

He didn't know if he even had a stove. ''If you're particular enough to want to use your own equipment rather than the stuff *Dream Date* sent, I think you should decide what we take.''

''Are you sure?''

''Absolutely.'' Talk about an inspiration. ''You are hereby appointed captain of the Keegan-Maguire Exploration Team.''

''I accept.'' She laughed, as if at some private joke.

''What now?'' He loved the sassy look in those butternut eyes.

''I was just thinking how much fun you would have had with Cheryl. She sure wanted to 'explore' with you.''

''Explore the mall—that was her speed.''

''She said she'd give you her phone number. Did she?''

She had, and he'd tossed it. ''Nah, the fireman got it,'' he fibbed.

''Firefighter,'' she corrected.

He'd give her that one.

While they'd talked, he noticed she'd been splitting the weight fifty-fifty. No way would he let her carry all that, not even for a little while. She was probably stronger than she looked, but her strength couldn't compare to his. He switched a couple of heavier-looking pieces from her stack to his.

"What do you think you're doing?" she asked in mock outrage, trying to snatch a hatchet out of his hand.

"Just trying to balance things like they ought to be."

"Women aren't weak, Pete. They carry their share of the load."

"You seem kind of hung up on that," he teased, dropping the hatchet back on her pile with a thud and, just for kicks, switching more things from his pile to hers.

But she put them back with great dignity. "I said it before, and I'll say it again. Women carry their share of..."

"The load," he chimed in. "Coach, you know, you really do have a problem with that."

"Deal with it." She motioned to the TV van turning into the parking lot. "We've got company."

His sister looked relieved to see them. "We got stuck on the freeway. I was afraid we'd missed you."

"You thought we'd leave without your send-off?" he teased.

She scanned his face and muttered, "You seem to be in a better mood than usual."

Sunny heard the familiarity between the two and knew she'd been right. Pete and Meggy did have an existing relationship. Had Pete's wife left because she was sick of him fooling around? Maybe Meggy wasn't as sweet and innocent as she looked. If she'd been taken in by another faithless charmer, there was no hope for her. She might as well swear off men forever.

Meggy pointed to a gigantic pine. "Brad, to establish the location of this segment, why don't you start your shot near the top of that tree, pan down, and catch Pete and Sunny playing peekaboo at the base. Okay with you two?"

Pete grinned. "Gee, Meggy, it's been a while since I played peekaboo. Refresh me on the rules."

Meggy butted him with her hip, bumping him off balance. "Don't give me a hard time, or I'll tell Mom."

Mom? They had the same ebony hair, the same dark, long-lashed blue eyes. They could be siblings. It would explain the silent communication she'd seen pass between them. The knot in her stomach eased. Pete wasn't like her ex after all. That was reassuring to know.

He came up behind her, put his arm around her shoulder and murmured, "Are you ready, wild woman?"

She looked up at his eyes, sky-blue and kind, eyes that would never let a woman down. "Ready," she whispered, stroking his cheek, loving it when he leaned into her touch and kissed her palm. Was he playing his role, or like her, letting need guide the way?

On the peekaboo shot, she flirted outrageously. With Pete it was surprisingly easy. He captured her, wrapped his arms around her waist and whispered in her ear, "Brad's got his camera on us. Give me a smoldering look. Show the congressman what he's missing."

Smoldering? Good grief, how did one smolder? It had to involve bedroom eyes. She could look sleepy.

"Wow," he breathed, "that's perfect."

His gaze dropped to her mouth, and then, as if he couldn't resist the draw between them, he lowered his face and completely covered her lips. This she could take for a long, long time.

"I think I'm going to be sick," Brad whined.

That broke the kiss.

"Watch your mouth!" Meggy ordered, "And just do your job."

"But we've got enough of this stuff. Let's move on."

"Brad, you don't seem to realize you're skating on very thin ice. I'm calling the shots here."

"Good! Call something besides this."

Jabbing her finger toward the trails, Meggy snapped, "Skate on up there and shoot their approach."

With an impudent salute, he asked, "Which trail?"

"Beginners," Meggy said.

"Advanced," Sunny amended, knowing Pete would prefer it, though it would be a stretch for her. "I don't want to hold this guy back."

Pete stroked her back and said, "Honey, the hike's not why we came. Meggy's right. The beginner trail will do just fine."

Before she could argue, he touched her lips with

a kiss, butterfly light, but possessive, the kiss of a longtime lover. Was he acting or not?

Of course he had to be. If he could play this game on her behalf, the least she could do was stay in character. "Darlin', I can't let you make all the sacrifices." She snuggled against his chest and rubbed her hands up and down his biceps. "My tough guy loves a challenge. We're hiking the advanced trail. Definitely."

She felt Pete's quick intake of breath.

"No!" Meggy cried. "That's too—"

"Let it go, Meggy," Pete interrupted.

"But, Pete..."

Pete threw her a silencing look, and she covered her mouth with her hand as if that were the only way she could oblige. Her eyes begged him to reconsider.

He shook his head and picked up his pack. What was going on?

"I hope you know what you're doing," Meggy muttered.

He passed her without a word, following Brad.

"If I haven't heard from you by seven tomorrow night," she called after him, "I'm sending somebody to find you."

With his sister so worried, why hadn't Pete told her the truth? They weren't really going hiking. The trail they chose didn't matter. But if Pete hadn't told her, there must be a reason. Maybe the less Meggy knew, the better her integrity was protected.

Still, there ought to be something reassuring she could say. As if they were going through with the hike, she said, "Meggy, we'll be fine. I'm not new at this, and Pete's an experienced camper. He knows what he's doing.''

''But he doesn't... Pete isn't...'' Meggy stopped, her mouth worked wordlessly.

''Meggy, what is it?''

''It's...nothing.'' Her troubled eyes followed Pete. ''I'm just a worrier. You guys have fun.''

It didn't ring true. The hooey alarm buzzed loud and clear.

Sunny adjusted her backpack straps, giving the woman a moment to share if she would. But Meggy turned and walked to the van, her self-assured, outgoing personality completely subdued.

Their path rounded a champion lodgepole pine that had to be fifteen feet or more in circumference. Pete waited with Brad at a small clearing, his irritation still obvious despite the smile he put on his face for her benefit.

One last time they performed for Brad's camera, acting as if they'd hiked for several miles, stopped for a rest and removed their backpacks. They sipped water from their canteens and pretended they couldn't resist a mountain-blessed kiss.

Naturally the kiss got the tingles in her stomach all worked up again. She barely knew this man but, given the choice, she'd take one of his kisses over a pistachio double dip anyday. They'd had—what?—two dates, and already she wondered if Pete Maguire wasn't God's choice for her.

Brad finally lowered his camera and said, ''Okay, kids, you're on your own. The sweet young things in L.A. are callin' me back, and I'm outta here.''

When Brad rounded the lodgepole pine and they

were alone, Pete enveloped her in a big hug, lifting her off her feet. It was celebration time.

Straight-faced, she said, "I think we ought to invite Brad over for a home-cooked meal."

"He can bring one of those sweet things from L.A."

"I'll make a cheesecake."

"I'll bring my mom. She can make pot roast."

They were just fooling around, saying anything, it didn't matter. What mattered was the connection between them, the humor, the fun. The awareness. Pete's eyes scanned her face, her eyes, her mouth, especially her mouth. Overhead a bird sang, and she thought she'd never been happier.

He lowered his head. Ripples of excitement swept through her body.

"There's no audience." Emotion made his voice husky.

"Just you and me," she whispered, her eyes locked on his mouth.

"We didn't expect this."

"No, but it feels right."

His kiss was soft, gentle, a perfect match with hers. He gathered her in his arms, pulled her close and kissed her as thoroughly as he had when the camera recorded it all, as if he really needed her.

One minute more and she'd forget the values she held dear. She lifted her mouth, but kept her eyes closed and her arms wrapped around him. It wasn't easy to let him go.

He took a deep breath and smoothed her hair, that same little intimacy she'd noticed before. Cupping her face in both hands, he whispered, "Where do we go from here, Sunny?"

Leaving this beautiful place had no appeal. A pizza, a movie and then to their separate homes for the night? That was better than nothing, but why settle for less when there was so much better?

"I've got an idea," she said, confident he'd love her choice.

"Whatever it is, you're still buying," he said with a grin.

"No problem. It won't cost much."

"It won't cost me at all. If you've changed your mind about pizza, just remember you said it was your treat."

She laughed shyly. "Then here's my treat. I'd like us to do the hike just as *Dream Date* planned."

Pete felt sick to his stomach. Her golden brown eyes sparkled with happy anticipation. And why not? She had a right to think he'd be pleased. On national TV he'd declared how much he loved all this. She was giving him exactly what she thought he would want.

This was the moment he should confess. How hard could it be? He'd admitted he didn't like cheesecake. She'd admitted she couldn't boil water. She didn't have a pickup, and he'd never explored in his life. It was no big deal. He'd just tell her, and she'd laugh about it. And then they'd go get the pizza.

But what if she said she'd teach him to camp? And she would. She loved this. She'd want to share it.

Then he'd have to get totally honest and tell her

about his bum hip. Again, no big deal. Sunny was the kind of person who took bad news in stride. He knew what her reaction would be. She'd feel sorry for him, but it wouldn't be pity. The woman could cope.

Go ahead. Just say, "Sunny, this could cost me dearly. Like, maybe a month in rehab. Even a permanent setback." He'd bet anything she'd even admire him for his honesty, his ability to share his fears, his trust in her.

Go ahead, he told himself again, sterner this time, tougher, meaner. Insistent. Tell her.

But he couldn't. There was just no way he could tell this pretty woman he wasn't the man she thought him to be.

# Chapter Five

"Let's do it." Solemn as a judge, Pete picked up his pack and looked up the trail.

It wasn't the reaction she'd expected. "Pete, we don't have to. If you'd rather—"

"No," he broke in. "It's a great idea. You take the lead."

Puzzled, she moved up the trail. This was no wildly enthusiastic guy, thrilled with another chance to camp and explore.

He'd been this way that first night in the producer's office when he'd warned her he would be "a lousy date." And there was that moment at her house when he'd tried to end the date before they'd eaten dinner. The rest of the time he'd been wonderful—fun, caring, protective, respectful. So what if she now had to add "a little moody"? Nobody was perfect.

The way he insisted that she take the lead and set the pace was especially thoughtful. A guy as strong and athletic-looking as Pete could run off and leave her with her tongue hanging out. She could add "considerate" to his list of good qualities.

Her competitive nature made her want to move along fast enough to impress him. Though she wasn't in the physical condition she'd been in when she played college basketball, she got plenty of exercise teaching and coaching.

At the pace she set, the first incline didn't allow for conversation. She'd rather hike slower and talk, but she didn't want Pete to think she was a wimp. Pride pushed her on.

When the path leveled off at a scenic overlook, Sunny stopped to catch her breath. She'd been so intent on covering ground that she hadn't paid attention to the trail behind her. When she saw how far behind Pete was, she felt like a kid who'd used the wrong fork at dinner. She might have known racing to the top wouldn't impress a serious hiker.

Pete had picked up a fallen branch and was using it as a walking stick, moving along in a leisurely fashion, examining his surroundings with great interest. Was he annoyed that she'd rabbited up the incline?

When he saw she was watching him, he raised his stick in a salute and sent her one of those approving smiles. It made her so relieved and happy. A lousy date? Pete Maguire was anything but that.

Pete lowered his stick from the casual salute and thought he might take up acting. The way Sunny had laughed at his salute, she couldn't suspect the hike had already started to get to him.

When he'd spied the fallen branch, it had seemed

a gift from heaven. It helped him feel steadier on the uneven terrain and gave him an excuse for his pace.

He'd had time for second thoughts. And third and fourth. He might have managed the beginner trail, maybe even the intermediate, but not this one. The elevation of this trail had no mercy on a bad hip. If he had a cellular phone, he'd call rehab right now and reserve a bed.

Back there he'd get little sympathy. There were guys who would give all they owned for the recovery he'd made. They'd think he was a fool to jeopardize his progress. And they'd be absolutely right.

When he finally caught up to her, she said, "I'm embarrassed. I took off like a rabbit, didn't I?"

She was making this easy. All he had to do was get a little creative in the excuse-making department. "I do the same thing if I don't use a stick as a gimmick to help me pace myself."

"Come to think of it," Sunny said brightly, "I remember seeing pictures of guys hiking the Alps, using walking sticks. Except they wore lederhosen."

"Mine are in my backpack."

Sunny laughed and the sound filled an empty spot in his heart. He settled himself on a rock and reached for his canteen.

"You've got the right idea," she said, finding her own rock for a seat. "I need to learn it's the quality, not the quantity, of the hike that's important. You've probably guessed I'm a competitive person."

"You wouldn't be much good as a coach if you weren't."

Those butternut eyes glowed. "You're a nice guy, Pete."

He used to be. He'd like to be.

"In fact, you're the first really nice studmuffin I've met."

"Stud-what?" he asked, puzzled.

"Studmuffin. You know, a good-lookin' guy the girls all go for. You're the real thing. The girls on my team said so. It must be pretty hard to take."

He didn't mind playing along. "Well, it is," he drawled. "You never know when you're gonna break some sweet thing's heart."

"I bet you've left a trail of broken hearts."

The way she said it, she might mean it. He couldn't let that pass. "Hey, I know we're just kidding around, but for the record, I've never broken a heart in my life."

"Not that you knew of," she said smugly. "All studmuffins are heartbreakers."

"Sunny!" She was pretty, teasing him this way, but exasperating, too. "No way am I a...one of them."

"You may not intend to be but, my man, you are. In fact, when it comes to studmuffins, you're state-of-the-art."

"Would you stop that?" She was having a good time, but he'd heard enough of this nonsense.

"Just don't let it go to your head." She waggled a warning finger at him.

It was The Face she was talking about, not him, and she couldn't know how much he hated it. In the long run, he'd have to get used to people thinking The Face was him, but today wasn't the day. She ought to know who he really was. At least it would stop her goofy talk about studmuppets or whatever she'd said.

He reached for his wallet, flipped to a photo and said, "Take a look at that."

She glanced at it and smiled. "A pretty bride between a couple of guys in blue tuxes."

"That's me."

She glanced at the picture again, frowning. "Which one? The bride, the young, clean-shaven man or the older one with a beard? You're not here. Or is this the point where you pull off a rubber face mask and become one of these people?"

"You've been watching too much sci-fi."

She chuckled, her brown eyes filled with delight.

So far, so good. She was handling this just fine. Now for the truth. "That's a picture of Lisa and me with my dad."

Her eyes widened and she looked at the picture again, then at him, and back to the picture. "Sorry, you're still not here."

"Look again. I'm the groom."

Sunny studied the features of Pete on his wedding day, trying to see the man she knew. The young man had Pete's half smile, dark hair, kind eyes and great build, but the face was totally different.

"Dad died recently. I dug this picture out because it was the only one I could find of him. He hated having his picture taken."

"I'm sorry for your loss, Pete." It seemed a pitifully inadequate thing to say, but she couldn't do better right now.

"That's okay."

She glanced at him to see if he meant it. He smiled back. She looked again at the picture. "This really is you?"

He nodded.

No one would call this young man handsome. Not even a loving mother. She looked up and compared Pete's classic Roman nose with the one in the picture.

"Checking the nose?" he asked. "Broke it twice playing football. How about the big chin? Just like my dad's. That was the face of one homely dude."

"Not homely! How can you say that?"

"Admit it. It's no stud...whatever you said."

"Well, no. But you were far from homely." If she were honest, she'd have to say, "not too far," but who needed that kind of truth?

"A couple of years ago," he said, "I got banged up in a car accident, and they had to reconstruct my face. I was drugged, and my mom who's a sculptor told them to give me a 'classic' look. This is it." He mugged, making such a silly face she had to smile. It was strange, watching him make light of such serious, life-changing injuries.

"Was it difficult, getting used to the change?"

"Who says I've gotten used to it? The guy I see in the mirror isn't me. He's just 'The Face.'"

Handing the picture back to him, she bent over and retied a bootlace. The lace wasn't loose, but she didn't want him to see her eyes right now. A lesser man might feed on a woman's pity, but Pete Maguire would hate it.

At least now she understood his total lack of egotism. It had been unfair to stereotype him as a worthless charmer just because he was as handsome as the one who'd broken her heart.

Searching for a positive comment, she said, "Your dad has nice eyes, just like yours."

He nodded. "I wish you could have known him. You'd have liked his sense of humor. He had his own construction company, and I worked with him, building houses."

"So, you really are a carpenter."

"Sure."

For once her hooey detector must have been wrong.

"My dad had 'Maguire and Son' painted on his truck the day after I was born."

"He must have been proud. Fathers are supposed to love having their sons following them into business. Did you always want to be a carpenter?"

The question bothered him. She could see it right away.

"Actually, I went to college to be an architect. It seemed a natural choice with my dad in the building trades and Mom an artist. But I dropped out after my sophomore year when Lisa said she was pregnant. I went to work for Dad, and we got married."

She wanted to ask about the baby, but that could be another sore spot.

He may have read her mind, for he said, "There was no baby."

But the promise of one got a young man with a promising future to the altar. Lisa must be a real jewel.

"And again, how long were you married?" she asked, trying to hide her contempt.

"Ten years."

It took him that long to wise up to Lisa?

"When I married, I married for keeps," he said softly, unresolved anguish clear in his eyes.

He was still blaming himself. She'd seen her friends go through the same thing—the ones who'd been left, not the ones doing the leaving.

"Do you want to tell me what happened?" she asked, offering an ear. It had helped her to tell him about Bruce.

He met her eyes for a second, no more, but that must have been enough for him to see she genuinely cared. Tracing his walking stick across the ground, he seemed to struggle for the right words. He could take all the time he needed. Explaining the end of a marriage was no easy thing.

"Lisa wanted out," he said finally, flexing his shoulders uneasily. "But they say it takes two to break up a marriage."

"Or three. Had Lisa met someone?"

He looked surprised. She didn't know why. It was a common scenario.

"She didn't meet him," he said cynically. "She'd known him as long as she'd known me. He was the best man at our wedding."

Ouch. That had to hurt. "Let me guess. Either you worked a lot of overtime hours which left Lisa lots of free time, or your buddy made lots more money than you did. Probably both."

He looked at her with awe. "Where's your crystal ball?"

"Don't need one. I watched the soaps when I was in college."

The half smile twitched, but he quickly sobered and said, "Lisa was raised poor. She seemed to need material things more than most. I don't think she could help it. I worked a lot of overtime so she could have what she wanted, but that left her alone."

"And your buddy with the big bucks was available with cash to spend on your material girl."

"Yeah," he drawled with narrowed eyes. "Intuition or more scenes from the soaps?"

"Both." On a visceral level, she felt an intense urge to make Lisa sorry she'd hurt this very good man.

"Lisa said I shouldn't take it personally. It was just time for an upgrade."

Sunny couldn't hold back a gasp. "What did you do?"

"Gave her the divorce."

"You didn't fight it?"

The barest move of his head said he had not.

"Do you wish you had?"

He shrugged. "I'm not much of a fighter."

"You were going to take on Brad."

"Yeah, but he was giving you and Meggy a hard time."

Pete would fight to protect his sister and a woman he barely knew, but he wouldn't fight for himself. She could identify with that. Hadn't she run from her parents and her ex rather than demand they treat her with respect? It wasn't something that made you feel very good about yourself. Peace came when you stopped running and gave the situation to God. She wondered if Pete knew that yet.

"Pete?" she began tentatively.

"Hmm?" He readjusted his position on his rock, getting comfortable, as if he didn't care whether they hiked any farther today or not.

"You said your accident was a couple of years ago. Your divorce was also a couple of years ago."

"Mmm-hmm."

"Talk about stress points. Yours must have rocketed off the chart."

He played it down, but she could tell she'd been right.

"Did you have God to help you get through all that?"

He studied a blue patch of sky. "Well, I'm here, so I guess He must have helped."

That wasn't the answer Sunny wanted to hear. Once Pete must have had a relationship with God, for he'd mentioned working with youth. Had he lost his faith or gotten sidetracked? People did over less than he'd experienced.

*Lord, if you have put me here, right now, to help Pete find his way back to You, give me the right words.*

"Want to know the funny part?" he said, breaking into her silent prayer.

"I can't believe there is a funny part."

"Well, I think it's kind of funny."

"I can't promise to laugh."

He smiled, his eyes saying he appreciated her empathy. "After the accident, I ended up with more bucks than Lisa could have spent in two lifetimes." His mouth twisted in a bitter smile. "But Lisa's not in on the joke. She doesn't know my income took a boost."

"And when she finds out?"

"I don't know," he said, stroking his chin. "I wouldn't be surprised if she didn't want another crack at being Mrs. Maguire."

"Will you take her back?" Sunny held her breath.

He laughed cynically. "No, but I wouldn't mind hearing her tell her husband that it was time for another upgrade."

Sunny joined his wicked smile. If Lisa could see how cute Pete was today, she'd really want him back, upgrade or not.

Cute? When had she started thinking of Pete as cute? Cute was for adorable, darling, cuddly people who touched your heart, not devastatingly handsome charmers like Pete and Bruce.

Pete and Bruce! That was so unfair. They were nothing alike. Pete would never use a woman's love to complete his own agenda. He'd never leave her wondering if he'd cared for her, even a little. And he most certainly would never expect her to swallow her pride, bury her hurt and return to him.

"Sunny?" Pete's brow was creased with concern. "What's the matter?"

She'd done it again. She'd dropped into the past, rehearsing old hurts as if she'd never given them to the Lord. How could she do that? This was a new day. Her future was in God's hand.

"Nothing's the matter," she said brightly, determined to move on. She stood, raised her backpack to her shoulders. "Ready for some new scenery?"

Pete watched her adjust the straps to her pack and wondered what had just happened. One minute those butternut eyes of hers had been popping with sass, the next they'd gone cloudy with pain.

"Why don't you lead this time?" she said.

Involuntarily wincing as he rose, he responded, "Go ahead."

But she shook her head and stepped aside. Pete took his time putting his backpack on. "Sure you don't want to lead?" he asked.

"Positive." She wasn't meeting his eyes. That bothered him. Whatever had taken her down was still on her mind.

The way his hip felt, he couldn't possibly move as fast as she had. But if they talked a lot, she might think he liked to hike at a snail's pace. Unfortunately, making conversation was not one of his strong suits. Like most guys, he could talk sports all day, but not the touchy-feely stuff women liked.

"Want to hear my first impression of you?" she asked.

He smiled to himself. Maybe he'd just let her do the talking. Women were better at that anyway. "Will it hurt?" he responded.

"I hope not. I just wondered if you noticed that I sort of blew you off at first."

Sure he had, but he did the chivalrous thing and fibbed. "You did? I was too nervous to notice."

"I apologize anyway. When I first saw you, and saw how good-looking you were…"

"Not me!" He had to stop her on that. "Just The Face."

She rolled her eyes. "Okay, but I deliberately blew you off, and I shouldn't have done that."

That bothered her? "Sunny, there was nothing wrong with that."

"But I didn't even know you," she protested, sounding upset with herself. "I couldn't get past your good looks. Bruce is an extremely handsome man like you and—"

He stopped her with a lifted brow.

"Okay, like The Face, and I immediately assumed you were like him. It was grossly unfair. I've been wanting to apologize and explain it had nothing to do with you."

He didn't need the apology. In fact, it embarrassed him, but she obviously felt better making it. He couldn't take that away from her. "Okay, but don't worry about it anymore."

"Now that I've seen the picture of the way you looked before, I especially want you to know it didn't take long for me to stop seeing The Face as just another good-looking guy. Pete, the real you shines through so strongly, your looks don't matter."

The conviction in her voice made him feel like the old Pete Maguire, and he almost touched his nose and chin to see if he'd gone back all the way. Maybe someday he'd get used to looking so different, but if he didn't, it was good to know it wouldn't matter.

"Forgive me for taking you at 'face' value?" she teased.

"Forgiven," he said, glad that the path here was wide enough for the two of them to walk side by side.

"The Face sure didn't seem to be a problem for

the other two girls on the show," she said, her brown eyes mock innocent.

He wished she'd forget about them, but if she wanted to play, he'd go along. They couldn't race up the mountain if they were joking around.

"Oh, yeah," he said, pretending fond memories. "Cheryl and what's her name, the brunette."

"Jacy."

"You sure? I thought it was Jani."

"No, Jacy. Definitely Jacy."

"Whatever."

"Whatever! Bruce would not only have remembered their names, he'd have dated them by now."

Pete shook his head, not understanding a guy like that. "With a girl like you wearing his ring, he was crazy to fool around."

They walked on for several yards before she said, "I was the last to know."

He knew what that felt like. "At least it was before the wedding, not after."

"You're right. I'm grateful for that."

After hiking silently for a few minutes, she asked what he thought about the latest trades among the NFL players, and that got the conversation out of the sensitive zone. Since she knew a lot about sports, there was plenty to talk about. He was grateful, for it kept him from thinking too much about the growing ache in his hip.

They stopped for a late lunch at a spot with a great view.

"Brad should have come with us," she said, munching on a nutrition bar. "I kind of miss the guy."

"Brad and his attitude," he agreed, swilling down tepid water.

"I thought Meggy handled him very well, didn't you?"

"Meggy did fine." He'd seen a new side to his little sister, and it made him proud.

"Meggy's your sister, isn't she, Pete?"

How had she figured that out? And if she had, had others?

"How could you tell?" he asked anxiously.

"I overheard her refer to your mother right after we got here."

"That was all?" That wasn't too bad.

"I also thought you seemed proud of her and rather protective."

"I am. Always have been."

"I could have used a brother like you."

He felt nothing like a brother to Sunny.

"So did your sister get you on *Dream Date?* Are you hoping to get noticed by someone for TV or movie work?"

He snorted. "Me! Are you kidding?"

"For modeling then?"

"With a face like this?"

She lifted her brow, and he rolled his eyes, remembering The Face. But he insisted, "Definitely no modeling."

"What then?"

"Meggy's in charge of selecting and supplying the contestants. When a last-minute cancellation put her in a jam, she begged me to fill in. Family members of employees aren't supposed to be contestants, so we pretended to be strangers. I didn't like it, but she was worried about losing her job, and she promised she'd never get in such a jam again.''

"Lucky Meggy. Not every brother would do that for his sister.''

The acceptance glowing in Sunny's golden brown eyes was heady stuff. Funny, how a woman could make a man feel taller, stronger and smarter than he was.

"I was really wrong about you," she said. "I even thought you weren't a carpenter like you said.''

She'd picked up on that? Man, it was time for more honesty. "You were right," he admitted. "I'm not a carpenter anymore. I don't need the work, and plenty of other guys do. After Dad died, we let the company go." He hoped he could leave it at that. "So you could tell I was fibbing, huh?''

"I was pretty sure you weren't telling the whole truth.''

"How could you tell?" he asked, intrigued.

"I teach school. I know hooey when I hear it. So if you're not a carpenter, what do you do?''

"Not much. On the show, I let the 'carpenter' thing slide because it seemed better than saying I was a beach bum.''

"You don't work? At anything?''

"Nope." Pete watched for the censure that any self-respecting person would have to feel, especially one who was a teacher and a Christian to boot.

"Exactly what does a beach bum do to pass the time?" she asked, a surprising lack of judgment in her eyes.

"Lots of things." He liked it when they talked

like this, fooling around. "I'm a professional, so I keep pretty busy."

"Uh-huh. Be more specific."

"Well, I watch a lot of clouds, noting their precise shapes and changes."

"That sounds exhausting."

"It is, and I listen to the seagulls."

"That, too? Wow. You just lie around all day?"

"Not always. Sometimes I sit."

Her eyes scanned his shoulders, arms and chest. "Well, I don't think you get those muscles building sand castles," she said, sounding like a teacher who was through with monkey business. "So what do you really do, Pete?"

Man, she was as bad as Meggy, digging until she got what she wanted. "I work out," he said evasively.

"And..."

"I visit with the neighbors."

"More..."

"I make a great pot of coffee."

She scanned his face. "You're not going to tell me, are you?"

He grinned at her. He was off the hook, at least this time.

"Okay, lunch is over, Maguire. On your feet. I'm tired of listening to this nonsense. We've got a mountain to explore."

He laughed and managed to get himself back on the trail without groaning. She made him lead again. How he wished he could stride out at a pace that would make her beg him to slow down, but every step was an effort. As often as he could, he stopped to reminisce about something or tried to get Sunny involved in a minor dispute about some pro athlete.

He even talked about his family, telling her about his otherworldly mother who lived and breathed art, and he described projects he and his dad had built together. He told her about Meggy's determination to have "And Daughter" painted on his dad's truck until she accidentally nailed her shirt to a roof when she tried shingling.

He asked about Sunny's family a couple of times, but somehow she always managed to change the subject.

By midafternoon, his hip hurt so much, conversation was too big an effort, so he examined foliage and rock formations, pretending enormous interest in everything. Every delay spared the needles and knives from jabbing into his flesh.

At home he had painkillers, and that's where he ought to be. Sunny was a great girl, wonderful, really, but trying to impress her had gotten him into this jam. He hoped she wouldn't take it personally, but this was no good. He was better off without her or anyone else in his life.

# Chapter Six

Sunny had never hiked with a person like Pete. Backpackers enjoyed covering a lot of ground. Each new vista over each new rise—that was the thing that kept them going. Pete, on the other hand, moseyed along, seemingly fascinated by every leaf and pebble.

By late afternoon, she knew something was very wrong. His face had a gray cast and his eyes seemed glazed. When they came to a spot where the trail ran close to a stream, she said, "How about stopping here for the night?"

"Fine," he said, not bothering to look around.

"It's not perfect. The tent floor will slope a bit, but we might not find a better place soon."

Indifferently he pointed to a more level patch and said, "What's wrong with putting the tent over there?"

She glanced at him to see if he was serious.

"Nothing, other than it's part of the trail, right in the path of the burros."

"The what?"

"The burros. They come barreling down the trail at night."

"Oh, right. How about over here?" he said, pointing to a flat area on lower ground.

It looked suspiciously like a creek bed to her. "Ever been in a flash flood?" she asked dryly.

He narrowed his eyes, scrutinized the flat area, then looked back at her. A pale replica of the half smile she loved crept over his face. "Just testing your knowledge of the great outdoors."

"Did I pass?" She pulled her tent out of its bag.

"Absolutely."

He reached for the tent poles, lost his balance and fell to the ground with a muffled groan.

"Pete!" She knelt beside him. "What's wrong?"

His eyes squeezed in a grimace, his teeth clenched, he said, "Nothing. I'm fine."

He was no such thing. If she had to treat him like one of the kids, she would. "Pete Maguire, you are not fine. Tell me what's wrong this instant."

He opened one eye and peered at her as if she'd lost her mind. Maybe she had. He had her plenty scared.

She tried again, this time with gentle pleading. "Pete, please tell me what's wrong."

"Women!" he muttered as if she weren't there. "If they don't get what they want one way, they try another."

"Men!" she replied, yanking on his shirtsleeve.

"They think they have to act tough when they're half-dead."

"I'm not half-dead."

"Then what? Three-quarters?"

He chuckled. "Maybe a quarter."

"I thought so. What's wrong?"

"It's just my hip," he said with disgust. "It got messed up in that car accident. Level surfaces aren't a problem, but this trail's pretty steep."

That's why he'd wanted to do the beginners' trail! "Oh, Pete, this is my fault."

"No, it's not," he said firmly.

But it was. She'd never believe otherwise, though the steel in his blue eyes said this was a bad time to argue the point.

"This is no big deal," he insisted.

Yes, it was. No wonder Meggy had been worried. Pete wouldn't be in this pain if she had listened. "Pete, I am so sorry—"

His silencing look cut her off. He wouldn't let her take the blame, and he wouldn't let her apologize. She felt miserable.

She must have looked it, for he struggled into a sitting position, took her hand and said, "Look, this is just temporary. Once I rest, the hip will be fine. Everything will be cool."

"Are you sure?" she asked, wanting to believe him.

"Absolutely."

That was a bald-faced lie. She knew it, but what could she do?

"Does it hurt really badly?"

"Nope. It's nothing to worry about."

If he would have admitted to some pain, she might have believed him. Total denial only made her more worried. How serious was this? Why take a chance?

"I'm going for help," she said, rising.

But he gripped her hand, not letting her move. "Not a chance," he said. His blue eyes flashed fire.

"But..."

"Sunny, give it up. I'll be fine. We'll get camp set up, get a good night's rest and tomorrow I'll be good as new."

If she didn't want to make him even more angry, she had to give in. It made better sense to play it his way for now. She could probably make it down the trail before dark, but it would be night before a rescue team or helicopter could come in. For the time being, she would make him as comfortable as possible.

"Pete?" she said, intending to improve his mood and, hopefully, draw his mind from his pain.

"What?" he responded tersely.

"These days, guys don't say what *we'll* do."

He groaned. "Just what I need. Another lecture." But she could tell he had grasped her intent and was playing along.

"We won't set up camp," she said in her teacher voice. "I will. The rest of what you said was okay though."

"What? The part about resting?"

"Yes, that was good."

He threw up his hands. "I surrender. I'm too beat to argue."

"Good." Taking his sleeping bag from his backpack, she propped it under his head. "Do you have medication for the pain?"

"Not with me."

What man ever planned ahead? She found her first-aid kit and retrieved nonaspirin tablets. Handing him his canteen and the medicine, she said, "Don't argue."

He grinned. "I won't. Thanks."

"Try to catch a nap."

Obediently Pete closed his eyes.

Sunny got the tent up, set out their cooking gear and gathered fallen branches, praying as she worked. As the temperature dropped, she pulled a sweatshirt over her T-shirt, added a down jacket and covered Pete with her opened sleeping bag. He seemed to be sleeping very deeply. She hoped that was good and worried that it wasn't.

Checking Pete's pack for the warmer clothing he would need when he woke, she knew they were in for trouble. The man traveled light. He had a windbreaker. That was it. No rain gear, no long underwear, not even a heavy shirt. She was no expert at wilderness survival, but Pete would be miserably cold at best, dangerously so at worst. If his sleeping bag wasn't heavily insulated, he would freeze.

She had a fire going and a simple supper ready when Pete woke. It was almost dark, and the temperature had dropped at least twenty degrees. She'd been watching him as he slept, noticing that his face reflected pain every time he'd moved.

From the way he rubbed at his neck, he must have developed a crick in it. She should have made a pillow out of something smaller than his sleeping bag.

"Feeling better?" she asked.

"Just peachy," he replied dryly, trying to smile.

She knelt beside him and massaged his neck.

"That feels good," he murmured.

"It's gotten a lot colder, and it'll be dark soon."

"Storm's coming, too," he muttered.

"You think so?"

"My bum hip thinks so. It predicts bad weather as reliably as the satellites. How long was I asleep?"

Sunny checked her watch. "About three hours. As soon as you eat, we ought to get bedded down for the night."

He levered himself into a sitting position, rolled over, moved to all fours, looked around until he located his walking stick and started to crawl toward it.

"Take my arm," she said, bracing herself to take his weight.

"That's okay. I can get up on my own."

"C'mon, Pete, let's work together on this. The wind's up, and it's getting colder by the minute."

"You're just full of good news."

"And you're stalling. Take my arm."

She knew how humbling it must be for Pete to need her help, but she wished he'd just take it. Everybody needed help sometimes.

But stubbornly Pete lunged to his feet on his own, swaying clumsily. She slipped her arms around him, holding him chest to chest, hoping his pride wouldn't push her away.

"Nice catch," he joked, putting his arms around

her, resting his chin against her brow. "Thanks for being there."

She felt at home in his arms and could have stayed a long time if she weren't so worried. Pete shivered, and she knew it was more than chemistry. Without anything warm to put on, he needed to get into a sleeping bag.

"Let's get you into the tent," she said, offering her shoulder as a crutch.

"Not yet."

"Pete, your shirt must have been wet with sweat when you went to sleep. You feel cold and clammy. We're talking survival here."

"In a minute," he persisted, "after I answer nature's call."

She chose a likely spot closer than the one she'd used, put her arm around him and said, "Okay, let's go."

"'Let's?' I don't think so."

"You need the help, Pete."

"Then hand me my walking stick."

"My shoulder's better."

"This is not a debate, Sunny."

The harsh tone in his voice said he'd die where he stood rather than accept her help. She handed him the stick.

"Thanks," he said, probably from habit, not real gratitude.

She turned to the fire, stirring it up to have something to do, willing him to go and hurry back.

But Pete just stood there, watching her. "I'm sorry you had to do all this work by yourself."

She shrugged. It had been the least she could do.

She wished he'd just take care of his personal business.

He shifted his weight awkwardly and raked his hand through his hair. "And I'm sorry I yelled at you."

She faced him, humbled by his determined consideration of her feelings, yet impatient, as well. "You didn't yell, Pete. You were frustrated. I'm ordering you around, taking charge, trying to make up for the fact it's my fault you're up here in pain. And you're standing there, being so nice I can't stand it!"

He pulled her up to him with one strong arm. "Hey," he said gruffly, "nothing's your fault. The last I knew, we were having a good time." He had a death grip on the walking stick, yet he was the strong one.

"I can't forget you wouldn't be here if it weren't for me."

"Maybe not, and I'm only admitting that this once, but, Sunny, I'm glad I'm here."

God love him, as miserable as he had to be, Pete was comforting her. And if he didn't stop it right now, she was going to bawl like a baby. "Thank you," she said, hiding her face in his neck.

"You're welcome." He hugged her close, stroking her arm, nuzzling his chin against her hair.

How lucky a woman would be to have the love of this exceptional man. He'd be a rock in all the tough times. Was God so good that He meant Pete for her?

A blast of chilled air hit them, and Pete shivered from the cold. She pushed out of his arms. "Hurry

back,'' she said, her voice choked with emotion.
''I'll have your dinner ready.''

He gave her a long look, but limped away without
saying more. She wished they were back in the valley with no reason to rush through these new feelings.

The temperature was dropping fast. It felt colder
now than it had an hour ago. She carried their sleeping bags to the tent and unrolled his. It was appall-
ingly thin. Surely there was an insert for extra insulation. She got her flashlight and was going
through his pack when Pete limped back into the
firelight.

''Caught you p-peeking,'' he teased through chattering teeth.

For once, his half smile held no charm. ''Pete
Maguire, why did you say your favorite outdoor activity was camping?''

''Same reason I s-said I liked ch-ch-cheesecake.''

''You've never camped in your life, have you?''

''What g-gave me away?''

''You're going to freeze. That's what! This sleeping bag belongs at a slumber party.'' Wasting no
time, Sunny unzipped the bag and smoothed it inside
the tent floor. Spreading her heavier bag over Pete's,
she was relieved to find the zippers compatible.
''Crawl in here,'' she commanded.

Pete struggled to the ground, grimacing in pain.
''Watch it with the orders, w-woman.''

Not only were his teeth chattering, Pete's speech
seemed slurred, and his hands shook as he tried to
untie his boots. Her heart sank. Though she'd never

seen someone with hypothermia, she'd bet her pay-
check she was seeing it now.

Helping Pete with his boots, she tried to remember the treatment. The main thing was to get him
warm inside and out. Her ski cap would keep heat
from escaping through his head. She had hot food
and drink ready. What more could she do?

He groaned as she helped him ease between the
sleeping bags. She'd always heard that men in pain
were big babies, but Pete didn't complain once.
When she put her cap on him, he even stuttered a
thank-you. Since his whole body tremored, she
steadied the coffee mug in his shaking hand with
her own.

Working that lopsided smile, he said, "Petey's a
big boy, Mom. Can drink by ownself."

"Sorry. Just trying to help."

"I'm c-c-cold, and my hip hurts like… It hurts.
But I'm okay, Sunny. Really."

Sunny knew better than trust his assurances. His
half smile was a poor imitation of the real thing. If
he was hypothermic, he wouldn't even realize it. It
was up to her to decide what he needed. If he didn't
stop shaking soon, she'd strip him down and warm
him with her own body.

While he drank his coffee, she checked the tent
stakes and secured their supplies. Huge flakes of
snow were drifting to the ground when she brought
Pete his food.

"How do you feel?" she asked, watching him eat.

"N-numb. It's really gotten cold, hasn't it?"

"I think you ought to get out of that shirt."

He looked as startled as a deer caught in headlights. "I'm not that k-k-kind of guy, Ms. Keegan."

"Pete! We're talking survival here! The sweatshirt I'm wearing is warm from my body heat. You'll feel warmer in it even if the fit is a little snug."

"You n-n-need your own shirt."

"Not really. Not with my jacket."

"Maybe you're r-right," he said, trying to unbutton his shirt with chilled fingers. "I've never b-been so cold."

She helped with his buttons, shrugged out of her own jacket, pulled her sweatshirt off, handed it to Pete and got back into her parka. Every action had the feel of urgency. The way the snow was coming down, they were in for a real blizzard. She'd never be able to go for help now.

By the time he'd eaten, it was pitch-black. Using her flashlight to see in the darkness, Sunny put both pairs of their boots in the rain fly. "Are you okay?" she said to the lump in the sleeping bag. Pete had scooched down so far in the bag, not even his head protruded.

"Just p-peachy," he said, his voice muffled in the bag.

She'd heard that before. Kneeling inside the tent, she fastened the flap and pulled off her jacket. Immediately she missed its warmth, but she could warm him better with only her T-shirt between them. In minutes the insulation of the sleeping bags would trap her heat and do its job.

She crawled in the bag, pulled the top over them

securely and tried to cuddle up to his back, but he was curled into a ball.

"Time to play Spoons, Pete. Stretch out. Let me warm you."

He mumbled something, but stayed as he was.

"You want the inside or outside?"

"N-n-neither," he chattered. "I—I'm too c-c-cold."

If he wouldn't cooperate, she'd take drastic action. Throwing one leg over Pete's body, Sunny climbed on top of him.

"Ow! Watch the hip!" Pete howled, twisting onto his back to redistribute her weight.

"I'm sorry." And she was, deeply. The guilt was piling up. "Pete, you've got to cooperate. Wrap your arms around me."

She guided his arms into place, and covered as much of his body as she could. Even through their clothes, the chill took her breath away as she cuddled her six-foot icicle.

"Brr! Wow! You are really cold!" she complained.

"D-d-do you usually go t-t-to bed with a g-g-guy on a first d-date, Sunny K-Keegan?"

"Second date. And only with the ones who have hypothermia." She rubbed his arms briskly. In a different situation, she'd have taken time to appreciate how well developed they were.

"S-S-Sunny, this isn't necessary. I'm not hypothermic. You d-d-don't have to do this."

Maybe not, but she'd never forgive herself if something awful happened to Pete. This was a crisis situation, and she would do what had to be done.

From now on, however, before she went hiking, she'd demand written certification that her partners had brains.

"S-S-Sunny, no kidding. I'm okay," Pete protested again.

"Just shut up, Pete, and appreciate this, because it's never going to happen again."

Pete was sure he was not hypothermic, but her body was warm and felt better than an electric blanket. He was cold. Really cold. But if he were dangerously chilled, would he appreciate the feel of her soft woman's body?

He had been intensely stupid to plan so poorly for this trip. Plan? He hadn't planned. He'd shown up. His irresponsibility had gotten them into this mess. They weren't in any danger, thanks to Sunny, but they could have been.

If anything bad did happen, he deserved it. Sunny, however, did not. She had trusted him, and all he had done was test her strength and scare her to death. For all her bravado, he knew she was frightened. There had to be a way to ease her fear.

"You d-didn't happen to bring one of those little handheld TV sets, d-did you?" That ought to catch her off guard. "I think the Angels are pl-playing tonight."

"We're here to commune with nature, not watch baseball."

Pete grinned in the dark. He loved her sassiness.

"But I like to w-watch TV before I go t-to sleep," he complained, still fooling around, although his chilled stuttering was unfortunately real.

"Get it through your head, Maguire. There's no TV."

"Then, y-you'll have t-to tell me a b-bedtime story."

"The Three Bears?"

"T-too scary when you're in the w-woods."

"Little Red Riding Hood?"

"That's another w-woods story."

"You're pretty picky. Maybe you'd better choose."

"Tell me the s-story of Little Sunny K-Keegan."

"That's a boring story."

"I'll be the j-judge of that."

She groaned as if she hated talking about herself.

"C'mon, I'm w-w-waiting."

"All right! Okay, once upon a time..."

"I l-like it already."

"You're easy to please."

He chuckled, tickled that he'd gotten her mind off her worry. "Once upon a t-time..." he repeated, leading her back.

"In the enchanted land of Beverly Hills..."

He grinned in the dark.

"There was a large castle where a king and queen lived. They loved each other very much and were busy from dawn until dusk entertaining royalty from all over the world and taking care of their subjects. Then, one day, surprise! A little princess arrived. She had the king's red hair and brown eyes and the queen's... Actually, she wasn't like the queen at all, which was a shame, for the queen was lovely and fair."

"You're lovely and f-fair," he protested.

"Who's telling this story?"

"You are, but g-get your facts right. It's a g-good story by the w-way."

"Not bad for a P.E. major, huh?"

"No, real g-good. Keep going." He definitely had her mind off his supposed hypothermia, and his shakes were almost gone.

"Everyone called the little princess Sunny, except the queen who demanded that people call the little girl Alexandra."

"Alexandra! You look like a S-Sunny to me."

"Are you going to keep interrupting?"

"Sorry."

"Princess Sunny-Alexandra liked to play in the tower, which was a playhouse in a very large tree. Though the queen wouldn't allow the princess to climb trees, the tree playhouse was so adorable, the queen couldn't resist showing it off to her friends who thought she must be an excellent mother."

He'd just as soon have his own mom.

"Sunny loved her playhouse, though she played school there, not house, except when Charles the chauffeur climbed up for tea parties and drank pretend tea with her from tiny china cups. Charles was her best friend. His wife, who was the cook, and her sister, Sunny's nanny, were dear friends, too. Almost like family."

The chauffeur, the cook and the nanny. They were the ones who'd raised her? That broke his heart.

"To the queen's horror, she discovered Princess Sunny would rather play ball than dolls. The king ordered knaves to build a really great basketball court on the castle grounds, and the queen didn't speak to the king for a week.''

Too bad the king didn't send the queen to the dungeon.

''The princess shot a lot of baskets as she grew up.''

''Career preparation?''

''I guess.'' He felt her stomach shake in silent laughter.

Man, it felt great, knowing he could make her laugh.

''The queen didn't like all that basketball-shooting, but the king liked the idea of the princess being a ballplayer like he was when he was a prince, so she learned to play pretty well. Sometimes the king came to her ball games—which she liked—but not as often as he promised, because the king was very, very busy.''

Pete didn't like the sound of that. He'd never be too busy to watch his own kid play ball.

''The princess went to college, played basketball, became a physical education teacher and began teaching and coaching. In January of her third year of teaching... Could I have a fanfare here?''

Fanfare? ''Tat, tat, tahhh!'' He gave it his best and was rewarded when her stomach shook again.

''The year of her twenty-fifth birthday, the king introduced the princess to a gallant knight in shiny bright armor.''

''Please, don't let it be Daniels.''

''But it was. Sir Bruce,'' she confirmed.

''Sir Skuzz,'' he corrected, and she snickered.

"Sir Skuzz was a great favorite of the king and queen for this knight had big royal dreams and wanted to be just like the king. To prove it, he showered the princess with lots of attention."

"Any knight would, with a princess so fair."

"The queen was ecstatic that the princess had snagged such an eligible knight, and the princess thought she was in love."

"Thought?"

"Yes, the poor twit didn't examine her feelings too closely, being so caught up in receiving unusual approval from her parents and being the object of this handsome knight's affection. It was only natural that when he gave her a big fat diamond, she accepted."

"Under those conditions, what princess wouldn't?"

"The princess helped Sir Skuzz campaign for the next year and a half. Once he was elected, the queen worked on a June wedding and the princess worked on her golf game. Royal wives don't play a lot of basketball, you know."

"I suppose not. Was the princess happy?" Her answer was important to him.

"Well, she thought she was."

That wasn't good enough, not by a long shot.

"Fortunately, she attended a very good church and got to know the Lord. After she jilted Sir Skuzz, things really got better. The Lord gave her a good job, and she became the famous coach of the San Josita Tigers who came from behind and unexpectedly won the regional championship. Ta-dah. The end."

"Can't be. The Three Bears is a longer story than that."

"You could have had The Three Bears."

"Heard it before. Your story was better."

Her head lay on his shoulder, and he nestled his chin against her forehead, knowing this very good girl deserved so much better than she'd had.

Why would a mother insist on calling a child Alexandra, especially when the child's big, beautiful smile and warm, butternut eyes made her so obviously a Sunny? How could any father put his work over a daughter who lived to please him?

Not wanting to stir up any more hurtful memories, but wanting to understand better, he asked, "You were an only child?"

"One and only."

"Any pets?"

"A dog lived at the same address."

"He wasn't yours?"

"Technically he was, but he lived in his own house and had his own fenced-in yard. Visits to Peppy were discouraged."

"Why? Was he a guard dog?"

"No, just a mutt with a cute, photogenic face. Mother didn't allow me to play with the 'dirty beast.' Only, he wasn't too dirty for me to play with when there were photographers around."

Photographers? Why would they want to take pictures of Sunny and her dog. "I don't get it," he said flatly.

She sighed. "This is turning into a long story."

"It's a long night."

"I've already told you more than I should have. This is not stuff I want people to know."

"Do you think I want them to know I'm an occasional cripple with a fake face who collapsed on a date and had to be taken care of? We've got some trust going here, haven't we?"

Against his shoulder, he felt her nod.

"Okay, then," he said, patting her back, hoping for her sake that this was a good idea, wishing for his own that he didn't feel so darn bad for her. "Start with the dog. Why were photographers taking pictures of you and, what's his name, Peppy?"

"Peppy was for photo ops. So was I. It's easier to get elected if you have a pet and a kid."

"Elected? Sunny, who are your parents?"

She sighed. "Sam and Eleanor Keegan."

Senator Sam Keegan? She hadn't been kidding with all that talk about royalty. The Keegan name was almost as big as the Kennedys. Senator Sam always made the shortlist of potential presidential candidates.

"Shocked speechless?"

"No way," he lied. "I was just thinking that I voted for your dad, too."

"That's okay. I think he does a good job. My parents both inherited wealth, and could have jet-setted through life, but they've genuinely tried to make a difference."

"And that's so noble it excuses their neglect of you?"

"They didn't actually neglect me," she said defensively.

He knew better, and it made him sick. Still, it

wasn't good to criticize a person's family. "Do you see them often?"

For a second he thought she wasn't going to answer, but she took a big breath and said, "I've only seen them once, the day after I left Bruce at the altar."

"Want to tell me about it?" he said, hoping Sunny would unload on him and feel better.

"Not really, but if you know this much, you might as well know the whole thing. If you're sure you want to."

"Absolutely." He stroked her hair, his heart already aching for her.

"Keep in mind, this was the day after I caught Bruce red-handed, but he had convinced them I had done him a great injustice. When I persisted with the truth, Mother said even if I weren't mistaken, infidelity was part of politics and a small price to pay for being the wife of a powerful man."

Pete let out a slow whistle.

"It gets worse. Daddy said, with me by his side, Bruce could make it all the way to the White House where he'd be a wonderful president. If I cared about my country, I'd stop pitying myself and help Bruce the way Mother had helped him."

"And you said...?"

"I said I just didn't feel that patriotic."

"Good for you!" He gave her a kiss on her temple.

"Mother was livid, and launched a personal attack. I'd heard it all before, so none of it got to me until she said Bruce only proposed to me to get Daddy's endorsement."

"People say things like that when they're mad," he said, downplaying the cruelty for Sunny's sake, but furious inside.

"When I thought about it, though, Daddy did announce his endorsement of Bruce shortly after we became engaged, and Mother didn't begin planning the wedding until he was elected."

"Coincidence," he said with more conviction than he felt.

"Hardly. They don't call Daddy a kingmaker for nothing."

"But a trade-off like that is so old-world. How could your dad guarantee a political office for Bruce any more than Bruce could be sure your dad would stick to the deal?"

"Men have gambled for higher stakes. Bruce knew how disappointed my father was that he missed his own nomination for president. If Daddy couldn't make it to the White House himself, the next best thing was putting his daughter there."

"Daniels would marry you to buy your dad's support?"

"Sure he would. He needs me—only not in the traditional sense."

How had she borne such deceit, such disregard for her worth? He cupped her head, nestling her face into his neck. "No wonder you went on *Dream Date*," he murmured.

"It turned out pretty good, didn't it?" Yawning, she snuggled against him. "I can't believe I told you all that."

"I'm glad you did." He shifted to his good side, rolling her over beside him. Her head lay in the hollow of his arm, and he wrapped his other arm around her middle. She laced her fingers through his, not something she had to do to promote shared body heat, just the natural act of a loving woman.

Wind howled through the pines, the sides of their small tent held fast against the blowing snow. Her even, deep breaths signaled she was out for the count. Man, she'd fallen asleep quickly. How could she do that, lying on this rock hard ground in the middle of all this...nature? Of course, her hip wasn't a constant ache, and she wasn't all worked up by a story of neglect and deception on the part of people she should have been able to trust.

Careful not to wake her, he nuzzled her hair. He was nobody special, just a broken-down carpenter with extra bucks in the bank, but as long as Sunny needed him, he'd be there for her.

# *Chapter Seven*

Give or take five minutes, Sunny awoke at six every day, eager to rise and shine. But waking on Big Bear was different. It was cold out there, and she might as well stay warm and cozy in the tent…in the sleeping bag…in Pete's arms.

Hello! Her eyelids flew open. This was a first, waking up with a guy. After twenty-eight virginal years, she'd have to say it made a nice change. Pretty great, in fact. One of his arms was her pillow, and the other tucked nicely across her middle. His legs cupped hers in true spoonlike fashion.

It was intimacy she'd never allowed, not even when she'd been wearing Bruce's ring. Being the daughter of rich, influential parents, she'd grown up questioning the motives of men. The first boy who'd liked her because she was a Keegan had been in kindergarten, or so her mother claimed. Even through college, she'd suspected every romantic move a guy made.

But Pete hadn't cajoled her into his arms. Necessity brought them together. Was it wrong to enjoy it a moment longer? Was it wrong to dream of a future where love was real and secure?

Maybe not. But the feel of Pete's strong male body shaped behind hers was mind spinning, the very kind of temptation she warned her girls about. If he woke now, when her early-morning inhibitions were so relaxed, and kissed her like he had yesterday, what would happen? Could she resist giving in to that? Would she want to?

She ought to. She knew what she believed in. First came trust, then friendship, then marriage. Total intimacy came with total commitment. That's what she wanted.

At least she did on an intellectual level, but wouldn't it be nice to turn in Pete's arms and let him kiss her into a beautiful new day? Groaning inwardly, she shoved against his arm, determined to keep her head straight and her body out of the sleeping bag.

But Pete mumbled a sleepy protest, tucked her back against him and slid kisses over her shoulder, nuzzling her nape. Trapped under his possessive, strong arm, she couldn't help but respond. The feel of his breath against her skin flamed errant tingles. She lay still, scarcely breathing.

He seemed totally content, just holding her in this intimate way, his touch so natural that sleeping with a woman was obviously no new experience for him. But then he'd been married for years.

What would happen if he woke right now and

found himself holding her like this? Talk about potential embarrassment!

Maybe she could deliberately wake him, but act as if she were still asleep. That would give him the chance to back off, believing she was none the wiser. It might work.

Pretending to be on the verge of waking, she stretched like a cat and audibly yawned.

She heard his quick intake of breath and knew he'd awakened. In a shot, he lifted his arm from her, then froze, not even breathing, as if he feared waking her.

Shifting, yawning again, she settled into "deep sleep," flopping her arm heavily across him.

Slowly, ever so slowly, he moved as far away from her as he could in the sleeping bag, taking great care not to "wake" her. If he had still been holding her, she couldn't have fooled him for her pounding heart would have given her away.

A minute passed, then another before she pretended to wake and rub the sleep from her eyes. Pete "slept" as if he were dead, his arm folded tightly against his own body, the very model of propriety.

Smiling to herself, she unzipped her side of the sleeping bags, and reached for her jeans. Stealthily she put them on, as if she were trying not to wake him.

Leaning over, she peered out the rain fly. Snow blanketed the campsite in pure white. Early-morning sun filtered through pines several stories tall, creating a mosaic of shadows and light. The sound of water rushing over rocks in the creek broke the quiet.

With her mind focused on getting Pete warm last night, she'd forgotten to tuck their bootlaces inside and they'd frozen to the ground. The boots were stiff and cold, but Sunny got hers on, all the while watching to see if Pete would officially "wake."

He didn't, and she crawled outside. Oh, it was a glorious new day. Standing there in the beauty of God's world, she raised both hands skyward, praising His name, letting joy fill her soul. There were valleys in life, but today she was on the mountain and glad to know the difference.

Down at the stream, she moistened a towel from her backpack and washed her face in water so cold, it took her breath away. Maybe a little freshening up was what Pete needed to "wake."

Taking the damp towel to the tent, she opened the fly and knelt beside him. Either he really had gone back to sleep or he played possum very well.

"Good morning," she crooned. "Time to wake up." She brushed the wet towel across his brow.

Pete's eyes flew open so fast, there was no doubt he'd been faking. She bit her lip to keep from smiling.

"Wow! That's cold," he complained, wrestling the towel out of her hands and dabbing his eyes with it. Tossing the towel back, he snuggled back under the bag. "Is it as cold as it was?"

"Almost. I'm going to fix breakfast. I thought we'd wait a while before starting back. It'll be warmer. Okay with you?"

He grinned. "You're the boss. Since I've admitted I don't know what the heck I'm doing, I might as well do what I'm told."

He looked so sexy, all sleepy-eyed and needing a shave. "How's the hip?" she asked, desperately hoping for good news.

"Great." His eyes shifted.

"Pete, you know I recognize hooey. Be honest."

"It's better," he insisted though he didn't meet her eyes.

She'd know how bad it was when they hit the trail.

It was nearly nine before she decided they should start back. The capricious Big Bear weather had changed again, and the snow melted rapidly. The trail would be muddy and, in places, dangerously slick.

Pete made a big show of being fit, but she saw how heavily he leaned on the walking stick. Could he make it all the way back on his own? She feared not.

Meggy had said she'd send somebody after them if they weren't back by evening, but that could mean another night on the mountain. She hated the idea of Pete suffering any longer than he had to. It would be better if she went for help. There was a clearing less than a mile away. If Pete could make it there, a helicopter could pick him up.

Sunny kept her plan to herself since Pete insisted his hip was "just peachy." He probably thought the downhill hike would be easier. It wouldn't be. Before long, reality would set in and he would give her no argument. She hated to think how much pain he would be in when that happened.

While she broke camp, she made him sit on a sun-warmed rock. He grumbled, but she reminded him who had appointed whom boss. Finally ready to leave, she said, "On your feet, Maguire. We're moving out."

He stood and saluted, mocking her drill-sergeant manner with his tilted smile. At least the smile was back in working order today.

"Hey, Sunny," he said softly, those bad-boy eyes of his sparkling with mischief. "Could you help me out here?"

Of course she could, but her teacher instinct said he was up to something. "Help you what?"

He beckoned her close, and then closer still, until she was near enough for him to catch her hand.

"What are you up to, Pete Maguire?"

His brows drew together in a worried frown. "I'm feeling kind of cold. I think it's my hypothermia coming back."

She hid a smile. "I don't think so. You're not shivering."

"I am on the inside," he complained.

Maybe he was. Feeling his thumb stroke her hand, she felt shivery herself. But she argued, "Your teeth aren't chattering."

"Sure th-th-they are," he said, making it true.

She frowned. "Hmm, it could be a relapse."

"That's what I th-thought."

"Think a little extra body heat would help?"

"It's w-w-worth a try."

She wrapped her arms around his waist, closing the space between them. His big arms enveloped her.

"How's that?" she said, resting her head against his shoulder.

"Much better." She heard the grin in his voice.

Familiar tingles danced up and down. His touch, his teasing, his kind understanding, they were exactly right. She hadn't known how much she needed this, and somehow she couldn't bear for him to know. It would make her seem pathetically vulnerable. So she said, "If you wanted a hug, all you had to do was say so."

"What if I wanted a kiss?"

For a second she couldn't breathe. Slowly she lifted her mouth to his. "Same thing. Just say so."

He took her face in both hands, staring at her mouth until she closed her eyes, paralyzed with anticipation.

He whispered her name and took her lips in a soft, tasting kiss, then another until she was floating, unaware of anything but this man and this moment. The world could go by. Just let her stay in his embrace.

When he pulled away and looked into her eyes, the warmth in his almost frightened her. She had no experience with feelings of this depth. The mere fact disconcerted her terribly. She'd been prepared to marry a man without knowing she could feel this?

"How's your hypothermia?" she quipped, seeking familiar ground. She couldn't have him see her confusion.

"All better," he drawled. The intensity of his gaze belied the laid-back inflection. "You sure know your first aid, Coach."

Was he consciously helping her to regroup? Could he see what an effort this was for her, struggling with strange new feelings?

She reached for her backpack and slipped it on. He looked around the campsite for his pack, but she tugged at his arm, pulling him toward the trail. He wouldn't find the pack, not where she'd hidden it.

He protested. "You're slipping, Sarge. I need my backpack."

"We'll leave it today. I packed light so we can move fast."

One dark, disapproving brow shot up. She'd expected this. What man liked changes, especially ones he had no say in?

"All right," he agreed cautiously, "but if we're only taking one backpack, I'm carrying it." The steel in his voice said he wouldn't put up with any of her equality nonsense today.

Again she expected that. Pete was too much of a gentleman to give in gracefully.

"I thought we'd take turns," she said, her fingers crossed. "Since I've already got my pack on, I'll go first."

"You don't need a turn. I'm twice as strong as you are. Give me the pack, Sunny."

"It's a new era, Pete. Women carry their share of—"

"Not today," he broke in, snatching at her pack.

She backed away, out of his reach. She'd counted on Pete's good nature to get them over this hump, but she'd underestimated the macho factor. She didn't want to make him angry, but if she gave in now, he'd be terribly embarrassed later.

She turned and started down the trail.

"Sunny!" he bellowed.

She didn't stop. Let him think she was headstrong, willful, obstinate, a brat. That was better than seeing him humiliated when the weight of the pack made it impossible for him to go on.

Pete felt as angry as he had during his first days at rehab. Now, as then, he had no choice but play the hand he'd been dealt. But he didn't like it, and he sure didn't like bossy schoolteachers. They were all alike.

He followed her down the trail, not too closely, but making sure he kept up. The descent was more difficult than he'd expected, and the snow hadn't helped. Once he lost his footing on a slippery tree root. Another time he'd have fallen in a pile of burro waste if Sunny hadn't called out a warning.

An hour into the hike, Pete was ready to apologize. Sunny must have suspected how painful this would be for him. With every step, the needles and knives bit deeper. Yesterday he had managed to ignore the pain until midafternoon, but today it was already a constant, relentless torment.

He did his best to hide it, but she knew. He could tell by the way she tried to distract him, pointing out unusual things, a tree here, a bird there, the way a person humors a tired, crabby kid. It was embarrassing, though it did help. A little.

She pretended not to notice when he stumbled or had to rest, leaning hard on the stick, but she missed nothing. He knew it. It was galling to realize the doctors had been right, warning him about stress of this kind. No wonder the settlement had been so generous. Step by agonizing step, he tried not to think of living on crutches for the rest of his life.

They came to a clearing where a bubbling creek

ran close to the trail. A few feet ahead a meadow lay beneath a crystal-blue sky. If his mind hadn't been so pain fogged, he would have enjoyed it. Under a pair of trees whose trunks had grown together, Sunny sat cross-legged, waiting for him to catch up.

"Ready for a break?" she asked cheerfully.

He could have told her cheerfulness was not a quality much admired by people in pain, but it wasn't her fault he hadn't had the guts to be honest with her about his disability.

Disability. Man, he hated that word.

She'd been a real trooper and done nothing but take very good care of him. If it killed him, he'd be sweet as pie the rest of the way. He ought to tell her how much he admired her spirit, her strength, her resourcefulness...and he would. Just not right now when he had to grit his teeth against the pain.

She had pulled her sleeping bag from her pack and spread it next to the tree. "Come sit down," she said, patting the pallet.

She looked pretty, sitting there, her coppery hair pulled back with little wavy straggles around her face. She wore no makeup, but she didn't need it, not with those beautiful brown eyes and that smile that made a guy feel better just to see her.

Painfully he dropped down and stretched out on the sleeping bag. "Sorry I'm not keeping up," he said, trying to sound good-natured.

"You're doing fine. It hurts, doesn't it?"

"Some."

She knew better. He saw that.

"You are one tough guy, Pete Maguire."

"Not so tough," he denied.

She didn't argue, not with words, just with her eyes.

"Interested in a snack?" she asked, opening a bag.

Pete held out his hand, and she filled it with gorp, the energy treat she'd introduced him to yesterday.

"How about some painkillers?" she asked.

Pete held out his other hand.

"Same amount as the gorp?" she teased.

He nodded, but she shook two tablets into his hand. He leaned his head against the tree trunk, closing his eyes, willing the pain away.

"Do you remember passing that meadow yesterday?" she asked.

He opened one eye. He did remember. They had crossed it just before stopping for the night after hiking most of the day. Had they actually covered less than a mile this morning? Already his hip was shot. How was he going to make it back at this rate?

"A helicopter could land in that meadow," she mused.

Pete opened the other eye. She was right. It was a little drastic, getting rescued by a helicopter, but if it meant the difference in walking or spending the rest of his life on crutches, he was all for it.

"Great idea," he said, hopeful at last.

"Wonderful! I was afraid you'd give me a hard time."

"Nope. Let 'em come and get us. I've got no pride."

She placed a gentle kiss on his forehead. It felt nice and loving and exactly like something Sunny would do.

"I figure I can make it to your truck and have the helicopter here in four, maybe five hours."

Not a chance! Let her hike out of here on her own? It was out of the question. "Forget it," he said firmly, tense, ready for battle. "You're not leaving on your own."

"Well, how do you think we're going to get the helicopter? Yell real loud?" Her big brown eyes questioned his sanity.

She could put a lid on the sarcasm. "You probably didn't notice," he explained, trying not to sound patronizing, "but Meggy expects us back tonight. She'll check, believe me. When I'm not back, she'll send help."

"But, Pete, your sister doesn't know where we are."

"She knows which trail we took."

"That's real specific."

"It's good enough. And better than you hiking by yourself."

"C'mon, Pete. Think. We'll be stuck here another night."

"Would that be so bad?"

"No, but you need medical attention, and I've got school tomorrow. I can't not show up."

"They'll excuse you when you explain you were stuck with a cripple," he said, hearing his bitterness and hating it. "You're not leaving here by yourself. End of subject."

Sunny rose to her feet and adjusted the backpack straps over her shoulders as if she hadn't heard a thing he'd said. "I need the keys to the pickup," she said, holding out her hand.

He ignored her.

"Fine. I'll hitchhike when I get to the road."

"No!" That didn't bear thinking about. If he couldn't bully her into doing things his way, he'd have to try another tactic. Speaking from his heart, he said, "Please, Sunny, don't go. I would go crazy thinking of you by yourself."

Her face softened, and he felt such relief.

"That's sweet."

It was going to be all right.

"But, Pete, you really can't go crazy in five hours, and that's all it will take."

Infuriating! That's what she was. Who was she to say how he'd feel? Didn't she care about his wishes at all?

"You'll have my sleeping bag," she said, patting his shoulder like he was a child, "and everything you need in the odd chance that something would happen and you had to spend the night here. I have what I would need in an emergency—my down jacket, food, water, matches, a knife."

His jaw hurt, it was clinched so tight.

"By the time you take a little nap, the helicopter will be here. Especially if you give me the keys."

Pete closed his eyes. If anything happened to Sunny, he'd never forgive himself. Yet, what choice did he have? She was going to have her way about this. He fished the keys from his jeans pocket and tossed them blindly in the air.

He heard her catch them, and he felt another kiss on his forehead. It may have seemed the same to her, but this kiss flamed his frustration. He closed her out, keeping his eyes shut, his face expressionless, wanting her to know how upset he was.

Her feet crunched across the pine needles as she walked away.

He didn't want his last words to her to be angry. "Be careful," he said gruffly.

She stopped. He heard her turn and take one step back. That's it. Stay. He sent the message silently, desperately.

"Please don't be mad at me, Pete."

She didn't want to leave him—that much he could tell. But she was going to anyway, and there wasn't a thing he could do about it.

When her footsteps died away and the only sounds were birds and the rushing creek, he opened his eyes and scanned the meadow. Sunny's bright hair was easy to spot. Without him to hold her back, she moved quickly. He'd been through many bad times in the past two years, but he'd never felt like such a failure. If not for his stubborn pride, Sunny wouldn't be alone on a wilderness trail.

He raised his eyes heavenward and prayed. "God, if you're really there, I need to know it. So I'm asking. Please...take care of my girl."

# *Chapter Eight*

It was early evening when Sunny parked Pete's pickup at the hospital and sprinted inside. The emergency room was teeming with activity and confusion. At the desk no one paid attention to her, and she wanted to scream. It had taken forever to get here, and she couldn't wait any longer.

"Excuse me," she said firmly in her best teacher voice.

A teddy bear of a man in turquoise scrubs looked her way.

"I'm looking for Pete Maguire. He was brought here by helicopter."

"You a relative?" the man asked, munching on a powdered sugar doughnut.

"No, a friend. We were hiking together on Big Bear."

"You can wait with his sister." He pointed to a corner where a cluster of males wearing assorted hospital uniforms hovered around Meggy Maguire.

Sunny couldn't tell if they were doctors, techs or what, but the E.R. couldn't be too busy if that many staff members could attend to one very pretty brunette.

Meggy spotted her and broke from the group. "I'm so glad you made it," she said, greeting her like a long-lost friend. "Thank you for calling me. Pete sure wouldn't have."

"How is he?" Sunny said, impatient to know.

"They're checking him out now. His own doctor is with him. This is where they brought Pete when he was, uh, sick another time."

"You mean when he had his accident?"

"You know about that?" Meggy looked surprised.

"Is it a secret?"

"It shouldn't be, but Pete's weird about it. None of his friends have even seen him since—" She stopped abruptly, covering her mouth with her hand.

"Since The Face?"

Meggy's blue eyes widened. "You know about that, too? Boy, you two must have gotten close."

"Your brother... He's quite a guy."

Meggy heard the catch in Sunny's voice and could have done a cartwheel. Sunny had fallen for Pete! Standing there in worn hiking boots, wrinkled khaki shorts and her heart on her sleeve, the woman looked wired and primed for one purpose, making sure Pete was okay. Finally fate had given her brother a break.

"Have you seen him?" Sunny asked, peering around the area.

"Just for a moment before he got them to kick me out."

"He did that?" Sunny's brow puckered.

"It's standard. Pete hates to have people see him in a time of weakness. He turns into an old grouch."

Sunny smiled. "You should have seen him when I insisted he lean on me to answer nature's call."

Meggy hooted so loud, the big guy at the nurses' station warned her with a raised brow. Cowering for his benefit, she confided, "My brother loves to be the protector, and he's very good at it. But when he becomes the 'protectee,' watch out. I'm surprised he didn't bite your head off when you left to get help."

Sunny chewed on her lip, not meeting her eye.

"He did bite your head off!" she said, instantly decoding that look. "Oh, Sunny, I'm sorry."

"I didn't mind," Sunny said, her brown eyes earnest. "He was in a lot of pain. He could have yelled all he wanted if it would have made him feel better."

This pretty redhead and her brother had connected! She looked at Sunny with potential sister-in-law eyes and liked what she saw. The copper-colored mane was a mess, there was a dirty streak on her cheekbone, a stain on her T-shirt and a scrape on her arm. She'd had too much sun and not enough sleep. But Meggy knew what her brother would see. He'd look into those big worried eyes, see the distress there and go straight to work, trying to make her feel better.

"When do you think they'll let us see Pete?" Sunny asked. "He was so upset with me when I left him. I've got to see him. I really have to."

The woman was a bundle of nerves.

"If I know my brother, he'll ask for a No Visitors sign even before he gets a diagnosis. They won't 'let' us see him."

Panic flared in Sunny's eyes.

Mercy, the girl was a mess. "Don't worry," Meggy soothed. "We'll get in."

Her new hospital friend, the intern with the intelligent, brooding eyes, strode purposefully toward them. "Your brother's going to be fine. He'll need some rest and a round of meds, but it wasn't much of a setback."

Tension left Meggy's body in a gush, and she turned to rejoice with Sunny. But Sunny's eyes were closed, her face upturned in silent prayer, "Thank you," on her lips. Scruffy as she was, the woman looked positively radiant.

"They'll be taking your brother up to ortho," the intern said. Leaning toward her, he added for her ears only, "I'll sneak you up once he's settled in his room."

She clasped his hand. "Thanks, Jon!"

"You were right about the No Visitors order," the intern said.

"I knew he'd do it."

She wasn't about to let Pete hole up in his cave again. She knew his tricks, and she'd known he'd pull this.

"If there's anything else I can do," the intern said, "let me know. You have my pager number."

"I really appreciate your help, Jon. I won't forget it, and I'll be calling you. You're going to make a fabulous *Dream Date* contestant."

\* \* \*

Pete was glad to be out of the E.R. and into a private room where they could post a No Visitors sign. Tomorrow he'd check out of here and into that new rehab place, a private clinic where nobody could find him, not even Meggy. He'd sleep away the prescribed time of idleness, courtesy of some nice little pills.

He should have had them on Big Bear, though if he had, he might have missed Sunny's bedtime story, and that would have been a shame. She was such a sweetheart. And funny, smart, brave…and something else. He couldn't think for the painkillers were already doing their job. Oh, yeah. Sunny was a really good kisser.

And she said he was a good kisser. He guessed he was, given the right inspiration. Lisa must have thought he was a lousy lover, so bad she had to find someone else. Someday he'd introduce her to Sunny.

The nurse finished settling him into the room, and he asked her to draw the curtain. A veteran at this, he knew how it was. The staff forgot and left the doors open, then people peeked in when they passed. Why wouldn't people respect a person's privacy?

In the E.R., Meggy had slipped in and driven him nuts, wanting to hold his hand, fussing over him. She knew he hated it when she got weepy, but did she keep the waterworks under control? She did not. As often as she got her way, it seemed he ought to get his when he was the one in the hospital.

Of course, he understood her fears. He'd even

shared them. When his doctor said there wouldn't
be any permanent damage, he'd about cried himself.
Two weeks of bed rest and some pills, that's what
the doctor ordered. It could have been so much
worse. Maybe he had a guardian angel of his own.

*God, it's a step of faith for me to believe You're*
*listening, but I think You must be. I don't know how*
*much You had to do with this, but it had to be a lot.*
*And You're still taking care of Sunny, right? I know*
*this isn't much of a prayer, but I'm grateful.*

He felt better, praying that prayer, though he'd
never done much of it. The Maguires said grace at
meals. That was about it.

He was glad Sunny had her faith. She needed all
the help she could get with that family of hers.

In the E.R. they'd told him Sunny was there and
wanted to see him. He would have liked to see her,
too, but only in a room with one of those trick mirrors where he could see her and she couldn't see
him. He'd give a lot for the sight of her pretty red
hair and that thousand-watt smile. Throw in a good
view of her gorgeous legs, and he'd donate cash to
the hospital.

He'd tell them to buy everybody a bed as comfortable as this one. It was the best bed ever, though
the stuff flowing through his IV might have something to do with it.

"Is he in here?"

He heard that and, even though it was a whisper,
he knew that voice. His bloodhound sister had
tracked him down.

"Over there, behind the curtain," said a man, his
voice soft.

Footsteps—three sets. One, rubber soles that squeaked on the tile; another, maybe sandals; and the third, boots that clumped, but not heavily. A hand wearing Meggy's class ring pulled on the curtain. Pete closed his eyes and tried to look comatose.

"Is he all right? He looks so pale."

That was Sunny! Bless her heart. If he wasn't such a bear about wanting his privacy, he'd perk up and reassure her himself.

"He's on some pretty heavy meds," the male said knowledgeably. "He probably doesn't even know we're here."

That was probably a young intern who'd big-shotted his way around the No Visitors order. He'd bet Old Red that Meggy promised to put the doc on TV.

"He knows we're here," she said. "His eyelids just fluttered." She jostled his shoulder. "Pete..."

He could fool her, especially if he just rolled his eyes back and let his jaw go slack. Well, not too slack, not with Sunny watching.

"Maybe we shouldn't disturb him," Sunny said. "But I wish we could have talked for a minute."

"He'll talk to us," his sister said with confidence.

"I don't know," the intern said. "Maybe later. He's pretty out of it."

"No, he's not," she argued, sisterly wisdom turning her into a real smart aleck. "Pete, you old faker..." She swatted his arm. "Open your eyes. You're not asleep. You know I can tell."

She could. It was true. And she'd never give up.

He opened his eyes and saw a vulnerable, weary Sunny who had done all she could to make sure he'd be all right. Her face was flushed from too much sun, and her big, brown eyes looked so uncertain of her right to be here, it almost broke his heart.

He reached out to her, and she slipped to his side, taking his hand. He rubbed his thumb over her long, slender fingers and remembered the way she'd laced them through his last night. He spread his fingers so she'd do it again, and, of course, she did.

"How are you?" she asked, her eyes searching his face.

"Don't worry 'bout me," he said, sounding gruff though he didn't want to be, not with her. "Are you okay?" he asked, trying really hard to be sweet.

Her smile was the great big one that he loved. The zing in his gut startled him so much, he gasped.

Meggy laughed out loud.

"What'sa matter with you?" he asked Meggy, surprised that his words came out drug slurred.

"You should have seen your face."

When she was like this, the only thing to do was ignore her. "Sisters," he said apologetically to Sunny.

Sunny stroked his forehead. "She was worried about you. We both were."

They didn't need to worry. He was going to be fine, and he wanted to tell her that, but he was so sleepy. Sunny's fingers were soothing, and he liked having her touch him.

The intern cleared his throat. "We should let him get some rest now. If you two get caught in here…"

"You've been wonderful, Jon. I'll call, and we'll get you scheduled for *Dream Date* right away."

Yup, the bloodhound had bought herself a buddy.

"Petey," she said from the foot of his bed, "we're going to leave so you can snooze." She squeezed his big toe and tiptoed away.

She could leave his feet alone, but it was better than having her kiss him. Sunny leaned down, her mouth coming toward his face. Her he wanted to kiss. He definitely did, and proved it by meeting her lips.

Her sweet kiss made his heart race, especially when the kiss changed from a comforting, goodbye peck into the real thing, a kiss that he wanted to go on and on, if only he weren't so sleepy.

"I'll see you tomorrow after school," Sunny whispered.

He started to say he wouldn't see her for a couple of weeks, but the drugs kicked in hard and he was out.

Sunny stood on the deck of her condo, stirring hazelnut-flavored cream into her coffee, remembering her vow two weeks ago that she'd learn to drink her coffee black just to be different from Pete's ex. Broken vows weren't good, but why keep the vow when she couldn't keep the guy?

As a judge of people, she was a real failure. She'd been so sure Pete was different. Granted, he was convalescing, but couldn't a guy rest with a phone in his hand?

Carefully she settled into her hammock with her coffee and Bible. These days she didn't feel totally in sync with God, not the way she liked. She still read the Word and talked with Him, but she'd think of Pete and a restless spirit would invade her peace.

Instead of keeping her mind on the Master, she'd
remember the smell of Pete's woodsy aftershave, the
way his eyes crinkled at the corners when he
laughed, how featherlight he'd stroked her hair, how
his kisses fired unrelenting yearning.

And she worried about him. She knew she
shouldn't, but she couldn't forget the pain he'd endured rather than tell her the truth about himself.

*Dear God, blessed and precious Lord, thank You
for being here ready to listen, ready to lead. Thank
You for letting me lean on You. Thank You for putting Pete in my life, even if it was for a short while.
I give him to You, Lord, to heal and to love. Be as
real to him as You are to me. Let him know Your
comfort, Your joy, Your—*

The phone rang in the house. She would ignore
it, but the answering machine wasn't on and it could
be Pete. Rolling out of the hammock, spilling her
coffee, she dashed inside and answered on the third
ring, "Hello?"

"Good morning, Alexandra."

She'd expected this call. "Good morning,
Mother," she answered, trying to keep the nervousness from her voice.

"It looks as if it will be a beautiful day, doesn't
it?" her mother said congenially. Eleanor Keegan's
manners couldn't be faulted, not when she wanted
to be nice—or had an agenda.

Matching her mother's civility, she said, "I understand we're to have relatively clear skies all
week."

"No smog, thank God."

Sunny drummed her fingers on the kitchen

counter, impatient with the preliminaries. It was her turn to volley. "Great weather for golf. Is your foursome playing as usual tomorrow?"

"Oh, yes. Nothing's changed. Not when we've had the same tee time for twenty years."

"Same group as always?" she asked, playing the banality game.

"Yes, all but Marsha. Barb's filling in for her."

Her mother's affable chitchat about Marsha's knee surgery was quite a contrast from their last conversation. It did no good to remember such things, but it was difficult to forget her mother's shrill castigation after the wedding that wasn't.

When her mother cleared her throat, Sunny went to full alert, recognizing the familiar launch signal.

"With Easter only a week away," her mother said affably, "I thought we should coordinate our plans for the day. Naturally we expect you to join us for Easter dinner."

Naturally? "Thank you for the invitation, Mother, but I'm spending Easter in Hawaii with friends."

"Change your plans. We dine at one."

That was abrupt. Bad manners, Mom. But maybe that was all a prodigal daughter deserved. "Sorry, Mother, but I've already made plans," she said, and braced herself for another tactic.

There was a pause, very brief, before her mother said, "Oh, Alexandra, I'm so sorry...."

Ah, the "dulcet tone." That was reserved for really hard cases. It was kind of cool, being thought of that way.

"I guess I should have called earlier." Her

mother sighed. "But we do so want you with us. Families should be together for holidays."

Then why hadn't she heard from her parents at Thanksgiving or Christmas? Easter at the Keegans' was no family affair, but a garden party for their inner circle, counting a hundred or more. Even worse, it was Bruce's crowd as well as her parents'.

"I'm sorry, Mother," she repeated simply, giving her mother nothing more to work with.

There was the slightest pause, which, of course, meant nothing, not when Mother had barely tapped her arsenal.

"Darling Alexandra..." her mother crooned.

Bad choice of weapons. "Darling" had lost its power from too many firings. Darling Pierre was asked to style her mother's hair on short notice. Darling Bridget gave her an extra half hour of massage. Mother would have done better with the minisob.

"It's just that it's been such a long, long while since we've seen you, and..." There it was. The minisob—just one, very faint. "We miss you so."

Sentiment careened in her heart, swamping her resolve. How could she let the suggestion of tears get to her, knowing it was only a tool? But her mother almost never cried. That's what made the minisob so effective.

In spite of herself, she said, "I miss you, too, Mother." They had never been close, but this was her only mother.

"It's time we let bygones be bygones, darling. Your father and I...we've been thinking about going to church this Easter."

Sunny almost dropped the phone. Easter for the

Keegans was bunnies and egg hunts. They attended church once in a while for voters' benefit, but her father never took religion seriously. Her mother ridiculed Sunny's relationship with God.

"Would it be all right if we went with you?"

Splat. They had her. The battle belonged to Mom. Manipulation or not, she'd do anything to bring her parents to the Lord. Readily she agreed to all of her mother's plans.

Ending the call, Sunny thanked God for this wonderful surprise and vowed she'd treat her parents with kindness and love. She supposed that started with thinking about what she should wear.

At her church, clothes didn't matter, but they did to her mother. What would Mom like? Perhaps her butter-yellow suit, casually styled in silk. She looked pretty good in it. And pearls—definitely pearls. Her grandmother's pearl-and-diamond brooch. How could she go wrong with that?

# *Chapter Nine*

The camel suede and navy leather bag came compliments of the rehab center to patients who checked in wearing their hospital gowns. Pete wondered what his dad would say to such luxury. Probably something about a man working too hard to waste money.

He hadn't much to pack—just a few clothes, his shaving gear and a roll of mints. Phone numbers from a cute little aide, a nurse twice his age and voluptuous Lauren Lemmon the movie star, he tossed in the can.

His one and only book would go in last. *"Be well in body and soul,"* read the words on the flyleaf, a simple wish from the chaplain on his first day here.

Pete had taken the book to please the man, not because he planned to read it, but after days of talk shows and ball games, he'd finally been bored enough to read a few pages. He'd tried to read the Bible before, but this contemporary version was different. It read just like any other book, and he'd been able to understand every word.

The more he read, the more he wondered where he'd gotten the idea God listened to one prayer and not another. And why had he thought God should answer prayer his way? After all, which one of them was God?

The truth in that book burned into his soul until he'd repented and made things right with the Lord. Well, almost right. He still had to face all those scriptures about forgiveness. A couple of times he'd told the Lord he'd forgiven Lisa and the lowlife who stole her away, but, once more for good measure, he prayed, *Lord, I forgive Lisa and…him.*

He still couldn't bring himself to say the bum's name though they'd been buddies since Little League. Words alone probably didn't count with the Lord. Man, he had a long way to go.

But he was on the right track. That was for sure. He felt better than he had in a long time. Stretching, letting the muscles roll across his back, he pledged full cooperation with his doctor's orders from now on. He'd learned his lesson, and he'd stick to his routine. Sunny would have to hike mountains without him.

Sunny. Now, that was a loose end. Would she want to see him? Did he have the nerve to find out?

A taxi was on its way to pick him up. It would cost a small fortune to go home by cab, but he had money in his wallet and plenty more in the bank. In fact, plenty to take a cruise or something. Well, not a cruise. Too many people. A trip around the world might be nice though. He could get a camera and take a bunch of pictures to look at when he was old and alone.

Wasn't that pitiful? A thirty-two-year-old guy thinking about his old age? That alone confirmed he was no studmuppet, or whatever silly thing Sunny had called him.

After the cab dropped him off at his house, maybe he'd get Old Red and drive by San Josita High. If he didn't spot Sunny there, he knew where she lived, although he might not recognize the place without the circus in front.

He wouldn't hang around in Sunny's life, making a pest of himself, but he was so hungry for the sight of her big smile, he felt like a stray mutt looking for scraps. It wasn't healthy, the way he thought about her all the time. Once he knew everything was fine in her life, he'd be able to relax and forget her. Well, not forget her, but let her be a nice memory.

As the taxi drove down his street, he looked at the houses, seeing them as a stranger would—say, someone like Sunny. Each small home had started out alike, built on a slab with a low-slung roof. Individuality came with an added vinyl canopy over the front door, shutters at the windows or a bit of brick siding. The yards were small, most with a patio in the back, and an extra vehicle out front, most sporting some rust or a ding or two.

It was a working man's neighborhood, one he'd been proud to be part of. It had been a big step up from the apartment Lisa had shared with her three lazy brothers, drunken bum of a dad and mother who taught her daughter to lie.

With a baby on the way, he'd wanted to do the

right thing, though it meant giving up college and marrying a girl who wasn't easy to please. His parents loaned them the down payment, and Lisa had fixed up the house real cute.

Once he'd gotten over the lie, it hadn't been a bad life. He'd worked long hours with his dad, come home to dinner on the table, played on a couple of baseball teams and kept a nice lawn. Lisa hadn't wanted to work, and he hadn't minded moonlighting on weekends to get the things she wanted. Some of the things. Lisa was never satisfied long.

But that was history. Lisa got their good car and their friends. He got the house, Old Red and a bucket of bitterness.

He opened the kitchen door with a key he kept in his wallet. Everything was as he'd left it, neat as a pin. In his closet the hangers were spaced evenly, an inch apart. He chose the blue knit shirt Meggy had given him for his birthday, changed into a pair of tan dress pants and socks, and slipped into loafers.

He guessed his hair looked okay and his shave was good. A dab of cologne wouldn't hurt, but just a dab, Meggy said when she gave it to him, unless he wanted the women to mob him. He'd settle for one redhead with long, gorgeous legs.

In the garage, Old Red came alive at the first turn of the key. Clean as a whistle, she was like new under the hood. He could have bought a new pickup for what he'd spent on her, but he didn't need anything better to prove who he was.

He knew the layout of San Josita High from his own high school days. Though he was more familiar with the baseball diamond, he'd been in and out of the main gym. He circled the school a couple of times, but drove off. He needed a soda—that's why he left. Not because he was nervous.

By the time he returned and got down to business, cruising past the playing fields, his window open, one arm on the ledge, trying to spot Sunny, the idea of being here seemed really stupid. Even if she were out there, how would he recognize her? She wasn't as big as a lot of those kids.

A piercing whistle, a sound he'd heard before, long and drawn-out, made him jam on the brakes. Two girls, one tall with an air of command, the other short and cute, came running up.

"You're Pete, aren't you?" the little one said.

The bigger girl palmed her head like a basketball. "Don't be asking the man dumb questions, Mouse. How 'ya doing, Pete? You come to see Coach?" she asked with a knowing grin.

He agreed, feeling awkward, chatting up teenagers.

"We were at the TV studio when you and Coach got matched," the little one said, smiling so hard, she might hurt herself.

The bigger one looked him straight in the eye. "I guess you know Coach is one in a million."

He wouldn't want to tangle with this girl. He nodded, approving her loyalty. "You're right about that."

"I think Coach really likes you," said the little one. "You're going to take her out again, aren't you?"

The bigger girl whacked her arm. "Mouse, what

did I tell you about keeping out of somebody's business? You got to excuse her, Pete. She hasn't had her medicine today. Do you want us to get Coach for you? She's over there at the second ball diamond.''

He grinned. They'd made this easy.

Sunny stood behind the catcher at home plate and watched another ball sail across the plate. It looked like Trevor would strike out again, even though the pitcher had thrown in two slow, well-placed pitches the kid should have hit.

The third crossed the plate just as easy, and she called, ''Strike three, you're out.''

''Aw, Coach, that ball was too low.''

''Take it like a man, Trevor.''

Sunny watched the sophomore mope to the bleachers. How was she going to reach him before school was out? Brilliant in math, a genius with computers, Trevor was small for his age and a constant complainer. The kids couldn't stand him.

''Coach!'' Leteisha and Mouse ran toward her.

They were Coach Harriman's students, not hers. They might be delivering a message. More likely they'd slipped off to visit.

''Coach!'' Leteisha called out. ''You're wanted on the next playing field.''

She hoped someone hadn't gotten hurt. ''Trevor!'' she called, pointing at him.

''What?'' he answered belligerently.

Nice attitude. ''Take over for me.''

A girl complained, ''Not him, Coach.''

''He's a geek,'' another cried. ''Don't let him ump.''

Speaking loudly for the class to hear, Sunny said, "Trevor's in charge. If anyone gives him a hard time, the opposing team scores a run."

Trevor sauntered to the plate and yelled, "Batter up."

She watched him long enough to see he was doing the job and having a blast. It was past time that kid had some fun in her class.

"Guess who came lookin' for you, Coach," Mouse sang, pointing to the road about fifty yards away.

"See that red truck over there," Leteisha said, nodding toward it. "It's your 'dream date' wanting to see you."

Pete was here? She shaded her eyes against the bright sun and spotted him waving at her. Joy bubbled in her soul. *Thank you, Lord,* she prayed silently, though she wanted to shout.

"You go on over there and talk with the man," Leteisha said, giving her a little push toward the road. "I'll watch your class."

Her students would be all right for a minute or two. She jogged toward the pickup. Pete got out of the truck and walked toward her, a big grin on his face. Praise God, he was walking without a limp or hesitation of any kind.

He'd dressed up to come see her. His broad shoulders filled out a knit shirt, and he wore dress pants that hung from narrow hips. His hair looked longer and shone in the sunlight. Best of all was the gleam in his eye. He was happy to see her.

Ten yards away, she broke out of the jog. The closer she got, the slower she walked. His pace, like hers, slowed as they neared. His eyes never left hers. There were no cameras, no pretense, nothing to prove.

Her heart raced as he scanned her face, feature by feature, then the length of her, from her sun visor to sneakers. It was at least ninety degrees in the warm spring sunshine, and windy besides. She knew what a mess she must look, but he seemed not to notice.

Grinning, he said, "You look great, Coach."

She felt a smile deep inside. "So do you."

She had so many things to ask him, so much she wanted to know, but those blue mesmerizing eyes of his stole every thought.

"I've missed my wild woman," he said, his voice low.

Her heart skipped a beat.

"Been doing much cooking?" he teased lightly.

"Just cheesecakes. How about you? Been exploring much?"

"Just the uncharted wonders of a rehab center."

"Must have been in a remote area, someplace without phones." That's it. Nag the man first thing. "I'm sorry—"

"No, you're right," he broke in. "I'm not very social when I'm in one of those places. Kind of like an old bear."

That's what Meggy had said when they'd worried together.

"Some people don't quite grasp the concept of solo hibernation. Namely my sister."

"It's only because she loves you."

His face softened. "She's my sister. I love her back."

Lucky Meggy. "We got together at a diner called Mom's and had pot roast in your honor."

"Yeah? We'll have to go there sometime."

He saw a future for them? She'd love that.

"I wanted to bring Old Red to meet you. She got her front grill bent out of shape because she didn't get to go on our date."

She laughed and gave the pickup a little wave "hi."

"Thanks for that," he said. "Red likes to be noticed."

"What woman doesn't? She sure doesn't look her age."

"Yeah, that's what I always tell her when she thinks I'm looking around at the new models. I won't throw her out just because something shinier comes along. That wouldn't be right."

He was kidding around, but the whole thing had an underlying edge that wasn't too hard to discern.

"I probably should have waited until this evening to see you," he said, glancing at the students, "but it was important to see you first thing. I couldn't wait to apologize for not telling you about…about my…that I shouldn't have done the hike."

"It's okay. You don't have to apologize."

"But I want to. I'm sorry, Sunny. I need you to know it."

A man who could say sorry. She'd take that over looks.

"I should have been honest. And I shouldn't have gotten mad when you said you were going for help."

"You were in a lot of pain. If anyone needs to

apologize, it's me. I forced you into taking that trail." Every time she thought about it, she wanted to cry.

He must have seen her eyes water for he tipped her chin up and said, "Hey, none of that. You have nothing to be sorry for. Absolutely nothing. You were terrific up there."

The praise, the comfort, the approval and protection, they came so naturally from this man.

"I'm glad you're here," she said, willing him to feel her welcoming heart.

A loud end-of-class horn sounded from the building speakers. She checked her watch, surprised that time passed so quickly. Blowing her whistle, she waved her students in.

"I probably need to go," he said.

Her heart contracted. She wasn't ready for him to leave. "Walk with me to the building?"

He nodded, and they walked slowly, letting students pass. She was so proud to be by his side, not so much because he was a very good-looking guy, but because he made it plain he was her guy.

"Did you see any of the tabloid pictures of us?" she asked conversationally.

He shook his head. "We made the news, huh?"

"Oh, yeah. You would have liked the one captioned Congressman's Ex Won't Go Back. It was perfect."

"Good," he said, satisfied.

"However, there was another one, a story about the senator's 'sex-starved daughter...'"

He stopped in his tracks, his eyes dark with horror.

"I guess you didn't know about my life as a nymphomaniac."

He made a strangling sound.

"No? Well, now it's out in the open. Take warning, Pete. No one man is enough for Sunny Keegan."

"That's such a lie!"

Sunny laughed. "Welcome to the world of celebrity."

A man wearing a uniform similar to Sunny's fell into step with them. "If this one can't satisfy you, Coach, I'm your man."

Appalled, Pete looked ready to grab the man.

"It's okay," she soothed, "Coach Harriman is just a big kidder."

The man gave her a grin and trotted off toward the building.

"I don't have much of a sense of humor when it comes to you and garbage like that," Pete said. "You shouldn't have to put up with it."

She would put up with worse if it got Bruce out of her life. "Next time Harriman messes with me, I'll let you get him. Okay?"

His glance said he couldn't make light of this one.

Leteisha passed by with Mouse. "We got everything, Coach."

"Thanks!" she called out.

Walking backward, Mouse said, "Hey, Pete, doesn't Coach have the prettiest legs?"

He laughed and gave Mouse a thumbs-up. "Those are great kids. They think a lot of you."

"Too much, maybe. The rumor mill has been active, with the tabloids and all. Leteisha decked a

student, defending my honor, and got suspended.
Mouse led the rest of the team in a walkout.''

"I've got to throw those kids a party. Tacos and
ice cream.''

"They'd love it.'' Some guys would say they
would do that, but, knowing Pete, he'd follow
through. "I heard from my mother this morning.''

"How did it go?'' he asked, frowning.

"Well, my parents are going to church with me
Easter Sunday.''

"That's good, isn't it?''

"It is, but I have to attend their Easter party af-
terward. Bruce will probably be there. I dread that.''

The frown deepened. "Would it help if I went?''

"You'd do that for me?''

"You know I would. I might not use the right
fork, but…''

"I'd never care about something like that.'' She'd
love to have him with her. "But I think I have to
go alone this time. My parents and I have some
things to work out.''

He scanned her face. "Sure?''

"No,'' she said with a little laugh, "but I'll be
all right.''

They reached the locker room door. The students
had gone inside, and they were alone. Framing her
face with his strong hands, he said, "You're tough,
Sunny. You can handle them.''

It was amazing how he could make her believe
better of herself. A few words, laced with approval,
and her confidence shot to new heights.

"If you change your mind and want some company, let me know. I could dust off my wings in no
time.''

# Chapter Ten

Pete poured hot coffee into his thermos and ignored his ringing telephone. The machine could pick up the call.

"Pete, I know you're there. Pick up."

It was Meggy, and he'd soon know if she needed help or just wanted to "sister" him. He tightened the cap of the thermos, opened the refrigerator and selected makings for his lunch.

"Pete! Would it kill you to pick up that phone?"

Low-fat mayo on whole wheat bread, three slices tomato, four ounces turkey. Make the sandwich. Put it in a zipped-lock bag.

"Pete, I just called to tell you Mom got married."

Sure she did. Two crisp pieces of lettuce, carrot sticks and bell pepper strips. Another bag. Deli dill pickle. Last bag. All the bags in the lunch box. Add an apple. Add a banana. Close the box.

"Mom's new husband is younger than I am."

Wipe the counter clean. Polish it dry. Check for streaks. Perfect.

He'd like to have a nickel for every time his ex called him a slob. Their last night together she'd complained about everything, from the way he forgot to put the toilet lid down, to the way he worked for his dad instead of going out on his own.

The complaining part was a pretty regular thing and he'd let the words slide, though he'd made a mental note to do better about the toilet lid. There hadn't been any use in explaining again that he stayed with his dad to learn from a master.

That this round of complaints was more serious hadn't sunk in until Lisa had dragged out luggage and started emptying her closet. Then he'd offered everything that usually made her feel better: buttered popcorn, a back rub and the new sofa they didn't need. And words. Especially words. Women loved words as long as you didn't try to solve their problems, though it sure came natural to help.

But Lisa's words he'd just as soon forget. *"I don't love you anymore."* That was a stab in the heart, then a wrenching hurt that lasted for months. He didn't want to hear that again. Ever.

"Pete, I'm still waiting." His sister's voice jarred him from the past. "I'm not going away. You might as well be gracious. Pick up the phone."

Some other time, Meggy. He had a schedule to keep.

Get the thermos. Get the lunch box. Open the back door.

Cute as a button in a bright red blazer and a triumphant grin, there stood Meggy, cell phone in hand.

"Just happen to be in the neighborhood, Meggy?"

"Where have you been, Pete Maguire? You know I worry."

Conniving, but caring. That was his sister. That's why he didn't boot her to the moon when she pulled stuff like this.

"I called you," he said. He had, once, to leave a message after he'd checked into the private clinic. "You knew I was okay."

"It wasn't enough. You didn't tell me where you were. I wanted to see you. So did Sunny. She called every day."

"I'm not Sunny's concern." He didn't mean it, at least not the way it sounded, but subtleties weren't important when he squabbled with his sister.

"I disagree," Meggy argued. "You made it her concern when you machoed up that trail without telling her anything."

The truth of that stung.

"You should have let us know where you were."

"But you'd have come, and you know I like to be alone."

She threw up her hands. "That's your problem! You always want to be alone. It's time you had a life, Pete."

He had a life, especially now, but he wasn't going to talk about it with his sister. "It's not your problem, Meggy."

"You're my brother. That makes it my problem.

C'mon, Pete. Let people back into your life. See your friends.''

"My friends?'' He couldn't believe she'd bring them up. His friends had known Lisa was having an affair, and none of them had told him. "Lisa got custody of my 'friends.'''

"That's malarkey. You cut them off without giving them a chance.''

"I don't see it that way,'' he said, edging around her.

She grabbed his arm. "Would it kill you to hang around long enough to finish a conversation?''

"I did.'' He shrugged her arm off and moved on.

"Well, I didn't.'' She grabbed the back waist of his jeans, and held on though he dragged her behind him.

"Let go of me, Meggy.''

"Not 'til you tell me where you're going.''

"The same place I go every day,'' he claimed, twisting free.

"You say you go to the beach, but that's the lamest thing I've ever heard. You got your sunblock in your lunch pail? Where's your cooler? Where's your towel? Give me a break, Pete. Don't insult my intelligence.''

"What intel—''

"Don't finish that.''

"—ligence?''

"I warned you!'' She balled her hands into fists and tried to land a punch anywhere.

It was a ritual they'd begun long ago. Dodging, weaving, laughing, Pete made it to his pickup untouched.

She kicked Old Red's front bumper. "When are you going to give this thing a decent burial?"

"Don't listen to her, Red," he said, patting the roof as he got behind the steering wheel. "She doesn't mean it." He turned the key, put Old Red in reverse and backed out, leaving Meggy standing in the driveway with her hands on her hips.

"Pete, wait!"

He hit the brakes. He knew that panicky sound.

She ran down the drive after him. "I almost forgot the reason I came," she panted, clinging to the frame of his open window. "I want to talk to you about the report-back taping tonight. You received the reminder in the mail, didn't you?"

He'd gotten it and wanted to show up as much as he wanted to repeat a surgery, but he wouldn't risk getting her in trouble. Besides, Sunny needed him to complete the job.

"You can save your pitiful little-sister thing," he said, "I'll be there."

Meggy's smile was the watery, grateful one he'd always suspected was as manipulative as it might be sincere.

"I bet you're looking forward to seeing Sunny, huh?"

Manipulative. Definitely. And she deserved to sweat for trying that on him. "You know," he said, as if he'd just thought of something, "there is this one thing I have to do before the taping that could make me a little late. But I don't think I'll miss the whole thing."

Her blue eyes widened. "Petey! Don't do this to me!"

Pete smiled and took off. In his rearview mirror, he saw Meggy stamp her foot. She wouldn't get so upset if she'd learn to mind her own business.

Rush-hour traffic on the Santa Monica Freeway was the steady grind one expected at this hour. Being part of it felt right. Like the other drivers, he had a destination, a purpose, a goal. He could have waited until later in the morning when the drive would have taken less time, but he liked it this way, riding along with his arm out the window, feeling the wind whip his hair, listening to his tunes, just being part of the crowd.

It didn't matter that his life had turned upside down in the last two years, that he'd lost his wife, his dad, the job he loved and his friends. When he saw the ocean, his spirits always lifted. His life was nothing compared to the vastness of the sea. If the Creator could keep all that power in check, he could take care of a sorry beach bum like himself, maybe even make him into something.

At one of the more modest beachfront homes in Malibu Colony, he turned into the driveway and cued a remote control to open the garage door. Parking inside, Pete went straight to the kitchen, plunked his thermos on the counter and transferred his lunch from the pail to the refrigerator.

Early-morning sunlight shone through skylights overlooking the living room as he headed upstairs and walked along the balcony. At the end, he entered the master bedroom and its huge walk-in closet. Stepping out of his sneakers, he placed them carefully on an otherwise-empty rack, removed his jeans and hung them on a hook. From a built-in drawer filled with beachwear, he chose a pair of black trunks.

Clad in the trunks and his T-shirt, Pete gave the empty tie rack a spin and checked his watch. Dithering with Meggy had put him off schedule, but not much.

Walking downstairs, he ran his hand along the stairway rail he'd installed five years ago. Though he'd worked on many upscale homes with his dad, this place was a favorite. It connected with the best part of his life. When he had more money than he knew what to do with and more hours than he could fill, the house had been available. For a million-five, it became his.

As he did every day, Pete poured a thermos-lid of coffee and carried it to the deck. Like a thousand watercolors of ocean meeting sky, the scene before him was sun-filled serenity. The rhythmic sound of the surf made him feel relaxed and alive at the same time. He sipped his coffee, relaxed in a lounge chair and wondered what the day would bring.

A school of dolphins might appear. He'd watch old men fish from the pier and pelicans bob for lunch. Bev Sapato next door would water her flowerpots and tell him the latest gossip her movie-producer husband brought home. Neighbors would pass and greet him by name. One was a rock star, another had his own sitcom. People were friendly out here, their back doors sharing the same ocean.

He finished drinking his coffee and lowered the back of the lounger. If he dozed a bit when people ought to be working, it wouldn't matter. Closing his eyes, he concentrated on the peaceful sound of water gently lapping the shore. He let his mind drift aimlessly. He hadn't a care in the world.

Except Sunny. She was unfinished business. He hadn't been this obsessed with a woman since his hormones raged as a teen. He told himself it was a logical reaction because he hadn't been with a woman in a long time, but he lied.

The wanting was for Sunny, and Sunny alone. He wanted her laughter, her sassy independence and her outlook on life. He wanted to see her beautiful eyes light up when she smiled, and he wanted to feel her touch on his brow.

To be very honest, he also wanted to sleep with his body molded to hers, his arms around her, their bare legs touching as they had on Big Bear. But it wouldn't happen. That was a fluke, a one-time necessity. That kind of closeness called for a man's heart, commitment, promises.

The promises he'd made to Lisa hadn't been enough to hold her. Without meaning to love her less than she needed, he'd failed. A man couldn't fail if he didn't try.

Chicken. That's what he was. A scaredy-cat chicken.

Afraid to go after what he wanted, playing it safe, letting the real world pass him by. But he'd never been a risk taker. At restaurants, he ordered steak and potatoes, nothing exotic. He didn't jump out of airplanes or dive into unknown waters. What he couldn't see, he didn't trust.

There it was: trust.

A couple of weeks ago, when Sunny talked about trusting God, he'd thought she was a little naïve.

Now he knew she'd been right on the money. How long had she been a Christian? Maybe with time, a person got better at trusting, though he couldn't see himself bungee jumping or anything stupid, no matter how close to God he became.

"Pete?"

The bloodhound? Not again. Her voice came from the beach. Ignore it. Maybe she'd go away.

"Pete?" She'd reached the steps to the deck.

Go away? In his dreams.

"What are you doing here, Pete?"

He groaned and peeled himself up off the lounger, marching toward the house. Meggy padded barefoot behind him.

"Answer me!" she demanded. "What are you doing here?"

Whirling, he jabbed a finger at her. "How did you get here?"

"I followed you."

"You followed me? I didn't see your car." He had checked his rearview mirror for it, several times.

She grinned. "That's because I borrowed a van. Gotcha!"

He ought to be furious with her, and he was. Unfortunately he couldn't stay mad nearly long enough when she was this happy with herself. Yanking a lock of her hair, he said, "Sisters!"

"Brothers!" she retorted with a kiss on his cheek.

He wiped the kiss off, scowling, hoping she'd back off.

But she beamed. "Are you house-sitting this place?"

Since it looked like his hideaway days were over,

he might as well come clean. "The house is mine. It was the last one Dad and I built before he died."

Meggy looked shocked. "You bought a house in Malibu Colony? What bank did you rob?"

"You knew there was a settlement from the accident."

"I didn't know you got this kind of money! You didn't act like it, and you live like a pauper. You let me rent you a truck when you could afford a place like this? Shame on you, Pete!"

"Renting the truck was not my idea."

For once she had no comeback. She sighed in contentment looking around the deck with its containers of flowers planted by good neighbor Bev. "This place is great."

Pete grinned, the happy pride of ownership making him glad to have someone to share his place with, even if it was his nosy sister. "Want a tour?"

"Sure, especially if it comes with a cold drink."

Pete stood aside, letting her precede him into the house.

"Good grief! It's a gym!"

It was, almost. Instead of filling the living room with furniture, he had splurged on exercise equipment to help his recovery. He hated those gyms where single women hung out, and he sure didn't fit in where guys were in love with the mirrors.

"Diet cola okay?"

"Sure." She followed him into the kitchen. "I see now why you didn't have a cooler," she said, laughing at herself.

He opened the refrigerator door and she peered

over his shoulder. Only a miracle would save him from another lecture.

"Uh, Pete…"

No miracle today.

"I know you've been in rehab, so I don't expect leftovers, but where's the food? Mustard, pickles, the standard stuff?"

When he didn't answer, she turned to the cupboards, finding them empty, slamming each shut a little harder than the last.

He crossed his arms, not liking this one bit, but knowing there was no stopping tornadoes, hurricanes or snoopy sisters.

"What's going on? There's not one dish, not even a broom."

"The cleaning lady brings her own supplies."

"Okay, but where's the dishes? The dish soap? What about all your vitamins? And your peanut butter? You can't make it without your peanut butter. It's like nobody lives here."

"Nobody does." He handed her a can of cola and carried one of his own into the living room.

"You don't live here?" She followed him like a shadow. "I thought you said you bought the place. I don't understand."

"What's to understand? I still live in Sylvan City. I come here to go to the beach and work out."

Her jaw dropped. Her blue eyes snapped. "You stay cooped up in that little house when you could be living here?"

"Sylvan City's good enough for me." When had Meggy turned into a snob?

"Good enough! What's that got to do with anything? A roof over your head is 'good enough' as long as it's paid for by honest work. We weren't raised to judge people by things. The only one who ever gave a rip about 'good enough' was…"

She stopped and stared at him, her eyes comprehending.

"Oh, Petey, if you're living at the old house to prove it should have been 'good enough' for Lisa, that's just pathetic."

She could stow that attitude and keep her opinions to herself.

"Don't you know by now that nothing would have been good enough for that greedy two-timer?"

It was true. Nothing had been good enough for Lisa. Not his job or the house. Not the amount of time he spent with her or the quality of life they'd had. He could still hear her voice, listing his shortcomings, justifying her reasons for leaving him. But he didn't discuss that with his little sister, especially when she stood there with pity on her face.

"There were a lot of things that bothered Lisa," he said, wanting Meggy to leave it at that.

"C'mon, admit it, Pete. Lisa was a pain. If you're still clinging to an old address when you could be here, you're just trying to prove a point. Unfortunately, the only thing you're proving is how much Lisa still controls you."

Pounding anger ripped through his body. Meggy had no business butting into his life, no business at all. His know-it-all sister had crossed the line. To make things worse, it didn't help realizing she just might be right.

* * *

Behind the pulsing neon heart on the *Dream Date* set, Sunny waited with Pete for their cue, wondering what had happened to the easygoing guy who'd gotten her through their camera-chaperoned dates. Standing here, he was as standoffish as a little boy forced to share space with a yucky girl.

Maybe he was nervous about going out there in front of the studio audience. That she could understand. The butterflies in her own stomach were having a party. Then again, maybe he was just here, doing his duty, helping her extricate herself from Bruce's life, yet wanting her to realize this was it for him.

If that was the case, so be it. Hadn't they both said they weren't ready for relationships? It wasn't his fault she felt differently now. She'd made it alone before. She could again. Still, only yesterday, he'd sounded as if he thought of them as a couple with a future.

"Are your girls here tonight?" he asked, breaking his silence.

"Yes, though Mouse is miffed because I wouldn't let her pick out my clothes. She says this looks like an old lady's dress."

Her peripheral vision caught him checking out the dress she'd chosen from her pre-San Josita wardrobe. There'd only been one that was sexy enough for the character she was playing, yet a step up from the leather miniskirt. A designer label, the style emphasized her figure without being too revealing.

"Mouse was wrong." His lopsided smile made an appearance. "You look terrific." His gaze lingered somewhere between her short hem and three-inch heels.

It was just a stab in the dark, but if there was such a thing as a leg man, she'd say Pete was it.

She returned the compliment. "You look nice tonight."

"Nice" was such an understatement. With his ebony hair freshly cut, his tanned, angular jaw closely shaved and his blue eyes just as kind and unconceited as ever, she could hardly keep her eyes off him. Dark jeans molded to muscular legs. A white shirt hung perfectly over his wide shoulders and powerful chest. The man was a genuine hunk.

"Nervous?" he asked, his eyes skittering everywhere.

"A little," she admitted. "How about you?"

"I'm so nervous, I'm about to be sick."

So that was it. How had she missed the tiny beads of sweat on his brow and the pallor around his mouth? "Are you going to be all right?" she asked.

He nodded. "It's the waiting I can't take."

Meggy passed them, escorting the program's chosen couple offstage. She must have known how Pete felt, for she patted his arm sympathetically and said, "You're on next."

Pete knew he was about to be seriously sick. Like the last time he was here, giant willy worms crawled in his belly. His heart pounded crazily, and breathing was a voluntary task. How did they get people to go on this show day after day? Maybe Meggy had been desperate for a replacement when she'd begged him to help out.

He sneaked another glance at Sunny. TV viewers

would do a double take when they saw her in this
segment. The first time they'd been on, she could
have passed for a working girl on Wilshire Boule-
vard. Tonight she was still a knockout, but Rodeo
Drive all the way. That dress probably cost more
than he used to make in a week, maybe two. Light
purple, the color of lilacs in the spring, it clung in
all the right places and had a short skirt that showed
off those fantastic legs. Her strappy high heels were
a big improvement over her hiking boots, and her
hair, shining like copper, curled softly around her
pretty face.

He'd told himself, after tonight he'd stay in his
safe, familiar routine where he didn't have to think,
where he couldn't possibly fail. Only, he didn't feel
like a failure with Sunny, and now that God was in
his life, did he need the routine? Today had been
rather boring. There had to be something better for
him.

He'd like to keep seeing Sunny, though she could
sure do better than him. From her description of her
parents' place, his Sylvan City house could probably
fit into their garage. She'd mentioned meeting the
queen of England, the pope, even Clint Eastwood.
Pete had seen them on TV. He and Sunny were
worlds apart, a distance not even his current bank
balance could bridge.

She was closer to the backstage monitor than he
was, and he leaned her way, as if he wanted to see
the screen better. She shifted her body aside to allow
him better vision, and he smelled her perfume,

something fruity that made him think of sunshine, peaches and cream.

On the screen Mike Michaels said, "A couple of weeks back, our audience matched a carpenter named Pete with a basketball coach named Sunny." Across the monitor flickered an edited version of the show when they'd met. "As always, our producers had Pete and Sunny's favorites in mind when they designed their dream date. Sunny said she liked to cook for her dates. Pete said he liked home-cooked meals. So, the first part of their date was Pot-Roast-At-Sunny's-Place!"

Pete watched himself drive up to Sunny's condo and walk to her door with the rose in his hand. He felt even sillier now, watching himself on TV, than he had then.

"Aw," intoned the emcee, "Pete brought Sunny a flower."

They edited right to the first kiss, and Michaels said, "Now, that's the way to greet a date, right, folks?"

Sunny murmured, "That looked like a pretty good kiss."

"Pretty good, nothing. It was a great kiss." It was the kiss that jolted him out of his solitary existence.

"And here's Pete helping out in the kitchen. He looks like he knows what he's doing, doesn't he?"

"I'm glad one of us did," she said softly with a giggle.

He loved hearing her laugh.

From Part Two of the date, they showed the playful peekaboo scene, their kiss under the big lodgepole pine and the helicopter landing on the hospital roof. He groaned, embarrassed at being portrayed as an invalid.

"I had to have my way about that trail," she whispered, her face drawn, her big eyes so sad, he couldn't take it.

"Hey, none of that." He put his arm around her. "We've already had this discussion. Okay?"

Her eyes searched his face. If his life depended on it, he couldn't have looked away. He wanted her to look inside his heart and see how much he wanted her there, needed her there.

"Ladies and gentlemen," Mike said, "let's welcome Pete and Sunny back to *Dream Date*."

The audience applauded and the stage manager cued them to go.

He couldn't move.

"Take my hand," Sunny whispered.

Like a man clutching hope, he took it, and once again walked into blinding bright light. Only, this time, he wasn't alone.

"They're holding hands, folks. That's a good sign."

The audience applauded as they took the sofa beside Mike.

"Tell me, Sunny," the emcee asked, "was your date with Pete all you expected it would be?"

"No, it wasn't. Not at all," she said, shaking her head, glancing at Pete apologetically.

Whoa! He hadn't expected that.

"You can see that Pete is a very handsome man..."

The audience applauded The Face.

"But I really dreaded going out with Pete. My experience with handsome men had been awful."

It sounded like she was getting ready to burn him, but he knew better than that.

"I assumed Pete was as conceited and full of himself as the last handsome guy I knew. That man—" she looked straight at the camera "—and you know who you are…"

"Oooooh," the audience responded, backing her up.

"That man was a complete disappointment. When I got matched with Pete, I was ready for the worst."

"Uh-oh, I'm almost afraid to ask. How did it go?"

"Mike, it was fabulous! Pete is the most wonderful man I've ever met." She turned and blasted him with that thousand-watt smile.

He swallowed hard.

"This guy doesn't have an ounce of conceit in his whole body. Unbelievable, isn't it, ladies?"

Applause burst from the audience. Pete felt hot color creep up his neck, but he didn't mind. This was for the congressman, not him.

"That's not all," Sunny continued. "Pete's the most caring man I've ever met. The only thing that's wrong with him…" She paused and glanced his way apologetically.

He wasn't worried. Much.

"Pete just doesn't realize how great he is."

"Ahhh," the audience approved.

His girl had poured it on pretty thick, but they

seemed to be buying it. He slipped his arm around her, cuddling her, playing along. Playing along? What a lie. He loved holding her.

Mike rubbed his hands together. "It's looking good, folks, really good. Pete, was the date all you expected it to be?"

Pete looked into Sunny's soft, butternut eyes. He owed her a lot. Even before she'd said all those nice things, he'd planned what he was going to say. "My date with Sunny—" he paused, letting tension build "—was the best date I've ever had. In fact, she's the best woman I've ever known." That was for Lisa and the congressman.

"Wow!" the emcee exclaimed.

"Sunny's everything a man wants in a woman. She's intelligent, understanding, fun to be with, and you should have seen how she took care of me when I was injured." He found the camera with the red light and said to her ex, "Any man who had Sunny's love and didn't cherish and appreciate her would be a real fool."

The audience applauded wildly.

"Mike, you can see how pretty she is, but inside, where it counts most, Sunny is even more beautiful."

"Whew!" Michaels exclaimed. "That's got me all choked up. I'm glad for you kids. At this time I usually ask if the date was a dream or a nightmare, but I think we already know. What was it, audience?"

"A dreeeeeeeam."

Sunny looked at him as if he'd just hung the

moon especially for her. Her eyes brimmed with tears, ready to spill any second. He bent his head, she circled his neck with her arms and he was smack in the middle of desire. The feel of her mouth, her arms, her sweet warm body—it was all he could ever want.

# Chapter Eleven

Bruce smoothed the side of his hair where bejeweled fingers ruffled it. He didn't like women touching his hair, but he had to put up with it. Too late he'd learned that Margo Price ratted her lovers out to her husband when they stopped making her happy, and too late he'd discovered her husband was a very scary guy. Everyone close to the senator knew Clive Price was on the staff because he'd do anything—snoop, steal, even worse.

For now he was stuck with her, but Margo would have to leave him alone when he got back with Sunny. That almost made it worth the hoops he would have to jump through.

"I hear Li'l Sunshine's joining us today," Margo said, angling her mouth on his.

"Easy, woman, before I forget there's not much privacy in a pool cabana. Let me get you a drink."

"Who needs a drink when I've got Brucey Daniels?" Margo giggled.

He gave her a naughty wink. "Brucey's not on the menu today, Margo. I'm saving myself for Sunshine."

"Then you should have gone to church with her." Margo laughed at her own wit.

"I'm not that desperate."

"Clive said she fell for that like a ton of bricks."

"I knew she would," he said, giving himself a mental pat on the back.

Margo touched up her lips. "After what she did to you, I can't believe you want her back."

"What I want doesn't come into it. Sam and Eleanor want her back! They treat me like the son they never had, but blood's still thicker than water. They want a marriage."

"I wouldn't worry about it. You're Sam's boy."

"Maybe so, but it's a long road to the White House. If Sam hadn't been waylaid by the morality crowd, he'd have made it himself. I need a wife who knows the ropes. Sunny's perfect."

Margo handed him a tissue. "If you want to be perfect yourself, you might want to wipe my lipstick off your mouth."

He grinned, complying. "How's that?"

"Lovely. Let's see what Eleanor's serving. I'm starving."

"You leave first. I'm going to mingle a while."

Bruce watched her meander toward a group sipping cold drinks under a white tent that shaded them from the hot California sun. In the gazebo a small band played the easy-listening music Eleanor Keegan preferred at these affairs.

Two young women wearing oversize Easter bonnets organized an egg roll contest for the kids of a hundred or so financial supporters and political operatives who chatted around the pool and garden. No one was eating yet, but under shady trees were tables laid with pink linen, silver and baskets of flowers.

One of Sam's aides approached the band and whispered something in the keyboard player's ear, probably an order to play the senator's theme song, for the band broke into it, and Sam emerged from the house, Eleanor on one arm, Sunny on the other.

They were a handsome family, waving at their guests, accepting applause. Eleanor's sleek blond coiffure and pink designer outfit suited her petite stature, but she paled beside the senator and Sunny. So alike no one would question their relationship, the pair had the same vivid coloring, slim build and magnetic smile. From here the senator looked the picture of health, and Sunny, in her yellow suit, was a bright beacon.

She seemed different than she'd been a year ago, more confident and sure of herself. She'd be an asset to his career, all right. He couldn't afford to mess this up today.

Sam and his advisers had planned this day as carefully as any campaign event. All he had to do was lay low, allowing Sunny time to get comfortable with the guests, most of whom she hadn't seen since the wedding. After she filled her plate, he would stroll up and give her a friendly peck on the cheek.

If that went well, they'd share a table with her parents, chat about her work at school and segue into how much they all missed her. When he got her alone, he'd grovel and promise anything to get her back.

If that didn't work, they would go to Plan B. He sincerely hoped they wouldn't need ''B,'' but bottom line, a man did what a man had to do. At least it would give them a photo.

To Sunny, it was déjà vu from the moment they gathered in the drawing room to this ridiculous parody of a royal family greeting their subjects. She stood by her parents, waving to people she thought she'd never see again. The past year might never have happened. She'd vowed she wouldn't get caught up in politics again, but if she were to have a relationship with her parents, this was the price.

At least she'd gotten them to church today. Mother hadn't been real happy about her wearing Grandmother's pearl-and-diamond pin with a casually styled suit, even it if it was silk, but everything else seemed to go well.

She hadn't been able to tell if her parents enjoyed the service or not. Daddy could beam at a crowd and mutter, ''Parasites,'' under his breath. Mother could rapture over a two-piece harmonica band as if it were the philharmonic. With them, you never really knew.

Greeting guests, shaking hands, exchanging hugs, Sunny was amazed at how easily the routine came back to her. She'd dreaded this, but either the Lord had smoothed the way or she'd underestimated the compassion of her parents' friends.

Mother was astonishingly gracious, and Daddy looked as if he would bust his buttons, bragging on how she'd coached her team to the regional championship. Too bad he'd missed every game.

Once she had taken all this for granted, but since tacos with the team had been her social highlight, she noticed the extravagant elegance. On the buffet table, an ice-sculptured bunny appeared to dance on fresh flowers. She leaned toward her mother and said, "I love the bunny, Mother. Top hat and all."

"Isn't he adorable. It's Fernando's work, of course."

Fernando? She wasn't in the loop anymore, but maybe next year, for the basketball banquet, Fernando could sculpt a girl doing a lay-up. That would knock 'em out in the school cafeteria.

Passing the dessert table, she noticed Cook had outdone herself as usual. Caterers prepared everything else, but nobody did sweets like Cook, and her mother left those to her.

There was pastry-covered brie topped with apricots and walnuts, caramel-almond crepes, berry and lemon tarts, meringue baskets filled with fruit, bunny-shaped sugar cookies and her favorite, a Royale Chambord chocolate-raspberry cake.

She smiled, knowing Cook had made it for her. The kitchen would be off-limits right now, but later there would be time for hugs and catching up with those who'd lovingly raised her.

Returning to her mother, she said, "Cook's goodies look out of this world. I want some of everything."

Her mother laughed gaily and gave her a hug.

Eleanor Keegan had never been a happy, hugging mother. Vicious quips and negative critique were more the norm. The way Eleanor was today, her girls would say aliens had stashed the real mom in a body pod. She'd say her mother may have found the Lord. That would be the most glorious thing.

"I'm filling plates for your father and me. Why don't you choose some food so we can sit down together?"

Sunny couldn't remember when her parents had eaten with her at one of these things, but it would be lovely, and she was suddenly starved. From the bountiful selection, she helped herself to several jumbo shrimp and a tender slice of beef brisket, passing a rack of lamb and a huge Virginia ham with their sauces.

"Make sure you have some of the lobster salad," her mother insisted. "That's new this year. And I had the caterers make the hot fruit compote especially for you."

Sunny was overwhelmed. Her mother had made an effort to please her. She didn't especially care for hot fruit compote, but she spooned a little onto her plate along with some of the orange-glazed carrots, a few asparagus spears and one of the tiny French-fried potato baskets filled with baby peas.

"Tell your father to stop socializing long enough to eat," her mother said, momentarily stopped by one of the caterers.

Sunny smiled. It felt good, being part of the family.

*Thank You, Father, for all of this. You promised You'd never give me anything too hard to bear. You said that morning comes after night, and You've brought me this far. I have confidence that You'll help me, no matter where the path leads.*

It was a little tricky, carrying her plate, walking down uneven flagstone steps in her high-heeled pumps and looking across the crowd for her father. She had just spotted him when she lost her footing and lurched forward awkwardly.

"Careful." A hand steadied her.

Bruce. She dropped her plate, and the sound of shattering china made everyone look.

Bruce took her in his arms as if he had the right. "Don't worry about the plate, babe. We'll get you another one."

"Don't touch me!" She pushed him away, breathing hard, embarrassed and angry. "And don't call me babe."

Her father stepped in, shielding them from curious eyes.

"What's the problem?"

She wheeled on him. "Daddy, I asked you. I asked you twice if Bruce was going to be here. You knew I didn't want him here."

"He doesn't have to be," her father said calmly, soothingly.

"No, I don't," Bruce agreed almost frantically, "not if it's going to upset you. In fact, I'm gone. See, I'm leaving."

As good as his word, Bruce vanished into the thick landscape of trees and shrubbery.

"I've got to sit down," she murmured, realizing her legs were very shaky.

Silently her father led her to a wrought-iron bench in the shelter of a tree where she used to play.

"I can't do this, Daddy. I can't go back to the way things were. I'm not that stupid anymore."

"You're getting yourself all upset for nothing. Bruce just wants to be friends."

"What happened?" Her mother hurried toward them.

"Sunny's had a little nervous spell. She just saw Bruce."

"Bruce? Where is he?"

"He apologized when he saw she was upset and left."

Her mother stared at her with contempt, her eyes so icy blue, Sunny felt the chill. Again, it was déjà vu. She was afraid because her mom was really mad. But she wasn't a child anymore.

"He left? A guest of ours had to leave because our daughter couldn't stand the sight of him?"

"Bruce isn't a regular guest," Sunny argued, fighting for equal ground. She would not let her mother beat her down.

"Doesn't that church of yours teach you anything about forgiveness?" Disgust contorted her mother's delicate features. "Why can't you let bygones be bygones? It's Easter, for goodness' sake! Surely you could manage to be civil today."

Guilt, layers of it, piled on Sunny's head, and she felt ashamed. Bruce had done a terrible thing to her, betraying her on their wedding day. The way her parents had supported him, and not her, was also bad. But was she any better if she couldn't lay her bitterness aside?

The Lord had His way of dealing with people. Bruce was God's responsibility, not hers. God gave people second chances, even more if they needed them. As His child, she should, too.

"I'm sorry," she said, her head bowed. "I can do better."

"Sure you can, Sunshine." Her father squeezed her arm.

"I'll find Bruce and apologize." In her prayers, she'd told the Lord she had forgiven Bruce. If she meant it, she ought to tell Bruce, as well. "I'll never go back to him, Daddy, but I do want to love him in Jesus' name."

"Let's not worry about Bruce," her father said, patting her hand. "We'll get some food, sit down, relax and enjoy the day."

He led her back to the buffet, and her mother followed, greeting people along the way as affably as if nothing unpleasant had happened. Sunny hoped her apology had placated her mother, but it wasn't likely. Her mother could hold a grievance forever.

The three of them sat down at one of the quartet tables, her father collapsing as if he were unusually tired.

"Try to eat something, Sam," her mother said, looking at him anxiously, though she only picked at her own food. "Oh, it's no use," she said, putting her fork down. "I'm so upset, I can't eat a bite."

"Let it go, Eleanor," her father said.

"I can't! Alexandra, after all you've put us through, we came to you, prepared to do anything that we might be reunited as a family. But you! You have ruined our last—"

"Eleanor, that's enough. I said, let it go," her father rasped between clenched teeth.

"Not this time. There is no time! She's got to grow up now and do the right thing. Oh, my head feels as if it will burst. Alexandra, pu-lease see that your father eats something." Throwing down her napkin, she left the table.

Her father's eyes followed her mother, and his sad expression broke Sunny's heart.

"I'm so sorry I ruined our meal, Daddy."

"It's all right," he said, patting her hand.

"I always upset Mother, but I want to please her."

"You please her, Sunshine."

She glanced at him sharply. For a man who could interpret the most subtle international nuance, that was blatant denial. But then, wasn't that his motto? Deny a thing long enough, and people forgot what was real.

"Instead of dwelling on the bad things, remember the good, like how much I love you. Never forget that, Sunny."

Her father never talked this way. It wasn't like him at all.

"I wasn't there for you much as you were growing up, though every politician sings that tune. But I believe in you, Sunshine, and I want the best for you. Always. Remember that."

She nodded, stroking his hand, willing him to see the love in her eyes.

He looked across the lawn where her mother crouched beside a little boy who was showing her how many eggs he had collected in his basket. "I want you to promise that you'll always be there for your mother, Sunny. Someday she's going to need you."

It was a strange thing for him to ask, but easy to answer. "I'll be there for her if she'll let me, Daddy."

"I know your relationship with her has been a bit difficult."

More than a bit, she thought, wondering at her father's introspective mood.

"But she does many admirable, wonderful things, Sunny."

"I know."

"I couldn't have made it in politics without her."

She'd heard him say that many times.

"I didn't come through for her, though." He sighed deeply, regret dark in his eyes. "She'd have made a great First Lady."

The White House had been her mother's dream as long as Sunny could remember. It had been ages since they'd talked about it, but she remembered the year her father almost won the nomination. Losing it had been a terrible blow. Away from the hubbub, secreted in their room, not really aware she'd been there, too, her mother had sobbed. Her father watched, grim defeat on his face, grieving more for his wife's loss than his own.

"Sunny, no matter what it seemed, my anger at you this past year hasn't been personal. I wanted your mother to have what she'd always wanted, even if she had to live her dream vicariously through you and Bruce. When you threw it back in our faces..."

"But, Daddy, I couldn't marry Bruce!"

"I know. You thought Bruce betrayed you, and you're as stubborn as your dad. I told everyone, 'Give the girl some time. She'll come around.' I still believe that, but, Sunshine, we're running out of time."

Her head spun. What was all this talk about running out of time? Would the pressure never end?

Leaning toward her, his gaze fiercely intense, he said, "If you love me…and I know you do…you've got to give Bruce another chance."

"Oh, Daddy, there's no—"

"Don't say no," he interrupted. "Give it some time."

But she could tell him right now. There was no way.

Shrieks from the children drew their attention to the terrace. A man-size Easter bunny wearing a top hat and tails danced merrily across the lawn, playing with one child and then another, making his way to a purple throne. Her mother lined up the children to sit on the Easter bunny's lap and have their pictures taken with him. As each child stepped down, a shapely young woman in bunny ears, leotard and tights presented the child with a basket of candy and toys.

One little girl seemed terrified of the bunny. Twice her daddy scooped her up and plunked her on the bunny's lap, and twice the child bolted, screaming hysterically.

"C'mon, Sunshine," her father said, grabbing her hand. "Let's show that little tyke she has nothing to be afraid of."

Still reeling from their emotional conversation,

Sunny trotted with her father to the purple throne, feeling more than a little foolish.

"Look, sugar," he said to the child, "my little girl's not afraid of the Easter bunny."

Sunny did her best to play along, allowing him to guide her to the bunny's lap. "Watch out, Easter Bunny," she said. "I'm a little heavier than the other children."

The silent bunny patted his lap and held out his arms, inviting her to have a seat. Gingerly she sat on his, or her, lap, trying to keep the bunny from bearing her full weight. But the bunny pulled her in snugly to his bunny body. He, and it had to be a he, was a very strong bunny, and affectionate, too. He laid his bunny head against her and let the audience know he liked his little girls on the mature side.

Knowing chuckles from the men in the audience made her grit her teeth. "Bunny," she muttered, "cut it out. Right now!"

The bunny shook his head vigorously and hugged her with both arms, his paws locked under her chest in a rough caress.

"Stop it," she whispered. "Don't hold me like this."

He answered with a tighter squeeze.

Not only was it the wrong answer, it hurt. "I'm not kidding," she muttered, beginning to struggle. "Stop it."

One paw shot up in the air.

That was better.

But, holding her just as securely with one arm, he used the free paw to pat her tummy!

"Ooooh," murmured the children. Even they recognized a naughty bunny.

She shoved against his arms, determined to break loose, but the bunny was stronger. She looked to her father for help, but he had his head together with a couple of men, all of them laughing, enjoying the show.

"Let me go, Bunny!" she cried, pounding on his arms.

The crowd laughed harder.

"Alexandra!" her mother called.

Gratefully Sunny looked for her in the crowd. Her mother wouldn't put up with this weirdo rabbit.

Spotting her mother, she felt such relief. For a second. Until she realized her mother's frown had her name all over it, not the bunny's.

"Your skirt!" her mother exclaimed in shocked disapproval.

The hem of her skirt rode high on her thighs, but what did her mother think she could do about it? She could use a little help.

The bunny raised one paw.

Oh, no. Not that again.

The children screamed, horror in their faces. She whipped her head around.

With his free paw, the Easter bunny had managed to remove his head. Without his head, he wasn't the bunny anymore. Breaking character was bad for the children, but worse for her.

The man's hair was disheveled and his face flushed, but the smile was as vote-worthy as ever. A camera flashed, catching her in the arms of Sir Skuzz, Congressman Daniels.

She could see the tabloid caption now: The Bunny And Sunny, Together Again.

"Let me go!" she demanded, stomping on his foot.

Pain registered up to Bruce's eyeballs, and he lost his grip on his prey. Twisting free, Sunny landed an elbow into his bunny belly. The punch didn't hurt, except for his pride.

What was she so mad about? She wasn't the one sweating like a pig in this hotter-than-Hades costume.

"Wear the bunny suit," her dad had said. "Sunny will love it." Boy, was her dad wrong. That picture better be worth it.

"Hey, boys and girls!" she said in a loud teacher voice, taking charge in an astonishing way. "Look! We have an Easter Bunny Man! Everybody say, 'Hi, Easter Bunny Man.'"

They did. With his bunny paws, he smoothed his wet, sweaty hair back, put a big smile on his face and answered, "Hi, kids!"

"Bunnies can't talk," complained one little smarty.

"That's right," Sunny agreed. "Easter Bunny, if you're not going to wear your head, you've got to try harder to look like a bunny. Can you do that?"

Look like a rabbit? Not a chance. He looked at Sam, knowing he'd get him out of this silly scene.

"Do it," the man mouthed.

Ridiculous. How low did a man have to stoop? It was a good thing he was an incredibly good sport.

Imagining the cartoon bunny, he raised his eyebrows high, opened his eyes real big and did that repetitious, smacking thing with his upper teeth against his bottom lip. The kids laughed, approving his efforts, and he got into the role, wiggling his nose and making quick rabbity head movements.

The crowd seemed to love it, except for Eleanor Keegan. So what? The woman had no sense of humor.

"He's a funny bunny, isn't he, boys and girls?" Sunny said.

"Yeeesssss," they all agreed.

"Poor Bunny looks so hot. I bet he could use a nice, cold drink." Sunny took a glass of ice water from a table.

He was plenty thirsty, but it looked as if someone had already drunk from that glass.

"Uh-oh, boys and girls, Bunny can't have this nice water. Do you know why?"

"It's got somebody's germs on it," yelled a tyke.

"That's right. But Bunny's so hot," Sunny crooned.

"Oooh." The children sighed.

He'd never seen her like this before, so in control, so comfortable with a crowd.

"Bunny, would you like this water anyway?"

Not really, but so what? A few germs wouldn't kill him. He nodded vigorously to make the kids laugh again.

"His big bunny paws might have trouble holding the glass. Who wants to hold the glass and give Bunny a nice drink?"

Hands shot up, and she chose a tubby boy who had Bully written all over him. The kid whispered in her ear, and Sunny nodded. Her grin looked positively evil as she pushed the kid toward him.

The kid held the glass high and tiptoed menacingly toward him, making the kids scream with anticipation. He knew the little brat was up to no good, but he also knew the kid's six-figure contributor dad. What was a little ice water compared to the kind of cash Tubbo's dad turned over to the war chest?

Actually, the ice water felt pretty good as the kid deliberately missed his mouth and let the water dribble down his chin and throat. But that wasn't enough for the brat, and ice water down a guy's back was a shock, no matter how hot he was.

Pure reflex made him swat Tubbo. Not hard. Certainly not so hard the kid should have yelled for his money-bags dad. The way the guy acted, stepping forward with clenched fists and a big, bad attitude, no wonder the kid was a bully.

The senator muttered in his ear, "Put that head back on and dance yourself out of here."

Hey, he wasn't the villain here, but he jammed the head back on. The band broke into a merry show tune, and he two-stepped in front of the crowd, working his way over to the bully's dad.

He didn't know where he got the nerve to shadowbox the guy, but the crowd loved it, especially when he let the guy sucker-punch him. With all the bunny padding, it didn't hurt. He pretended to reel from the blow, and the guy was all smiles.

Back at the house, he shucked out of the bunny suit and vowed he'd never let anyone talk him into putting on a costume again. That went for Santa

Claus suits, Mardi Gras masks and Uncle Sam hats. He was done with 'em all.

But Sam seemed delighted. Slapping him on the shoulder, he said, "You're a natural, son. They were eating out of your hand."

If Sam was happy, he was happy. "How about Sunny?" he asked. "I didn't see her after that kid dumped water on me."

"I didn't, either, but one of the boys said she hightailed it up to the house and asked Charles to drive her home."

"That doesn't sound good. Do you think we spooked her?"

"No such thing. She just showed a little spunk."

That had to be a dad talking. The bruise developing on his foot didn't come from a little spunk. "Could I be wrong, Sam? Maybe Sunny doesn't love me. What if she doesn't come around?"

"She will. This was only her first time back in the saddle."

"But she acted as if I were poison."

"Well, you hurt her, Bruce. Sunny was never a confident woman, especially about men, and it didn't help that she found you with that woman."

"There wasn't a thing I could do about it, but I'll always regret that, Sam." Bruce hung his head, genuinely sorry. That particular indiscretion had cost him dearly. "Nobody knows better than you how it is when one of those women goes after you."

The senator shook his head knowingly. "You're nothing to them but a trophy. But try to tell that to the public."

"Exactly. That bridesmaid practically attacked

me. I'd give anything if Sunny hadn't seen it and gotten the wrong idea."

Sam patted his back. "I know, son. It was a terrible case of the wrong place and the wrong time. But Sunny will come around. I know my girl."

"I miss her." Bruce let his voice crack, a little technique held over from puberty. It came in handy when he needed an extra punch of sincerity. "It's been lonely without her."

"Keep your chin up, boy."

Sam was more of a father to him than his own dad who thought all lawyers and politicians were crooks and had washed his hands of him long ago. Maybe Sam would back him without Sunny bearing his name, but why risk it? The European royalty had it right with their marriages of alliance.

If charm didn't work on Sunny, he had a few other tricks up his sleeve. He knew about her going on TV and the charade she was trying to pull with that out-of-work carpenter. That *Dream Date* episode would never see air, not even if he had to resort to some high-risk tactics with some very wrong people.

If all else failed and Sunny wouldn't cooperate, he had his new little girlfriend ready to step in. She was cute as a button, highly photogenic and eager to be a cookie-bakin' First Lady. Sam and Eleanor could still live their dream through him.

# Chapter Twelve

Sunny brushed her hair back into a ponytail and shoved a sun visor over her brow. The kids might moan about the end of spring break, but she was ready to get on with her everyday life.

Thank goodness she hadn't taken Pete to her parents' house for Easter dinner. Yesterday had been a disaster. They hadn't been ready to accept her, let alone a new man in her life. And did she handle it like the mature Christian she wanted to be? Hardly, though Bruce had seriously crossed the line.

But she'd learned a couple of things from yesterday. One—her family knew her too well. "We want to go to church with you" had been the perfect bait. She'd swallowed the hook, not stopping to think or ask the Lord's direction, just assuming anything that would bring her parents into God's Presence had to be His will.

Two—she'd do better to let God coach the game. How could she have forgotten to check with Him before she acted? If one of her girls didn't run the designated pattern, she found herself on the bench.

Grabbing her keys, she headed for the garage, but the phone rang. If it were Pete, there was no better way to start the day. Maybe she'd offer him a home-cooked meal. She made a great grilled-cheese sandwich. Or this could be the night they went to Mom's for pot roast.

The machine clicked on. "Alexandra?

*Thank you, Lord, for machines.*

"Have you lost your mind?"

Just what she needed to start the day. A psychiatric evaluation, compliments of Mom.

"We went out of our way to make things nice for you, and you ran off before I could tell you about Daddy's party. It's this Saturday night at the Crowne, a gala in his honor. Sam is adamant that you be there. It means everything to him."

Why? Didn't the photographer get a picture of her with Bunny Bruce yesterday?

"I know this is terribly short notice. You weren't invited earlier because, frankly, we didn't think you would attend. Then, just recently, the event has taken on special significance."

Only recently? She supposed her *Dream Date* escapade would need specially significant explaining.

"Alexandra, I have never begged you to do something for me, but I'm begging you now."

Good grief. Her mother had added a new weapon to the arsenal. And a powerful one, it was.

"Please, be there for your father. You simply have no idea what this means to him...."

Was that the minisob?

"I'll help you every way I can. Charles will deliver your dress. Pierre will do your hair and makeup. And Sunny…"

Her mother never called her that.

"Daddy says you told him you've forgiven Bruce. I hope, I pray, that he's right. More than anything, Sam wants the four of us to attend as a family."

The message ended, and Sunny slumped against the wall. She couldn't do that, but what could she do? She wasn't tough enough, or callous enough, to purposefully disappoint them, yet she didn't want to undo everything she'd proven by going on *Dream Date* in the first place.

She got in her car, headed for school and thought like Sam and Eleanor Keegan's daughter, considering one tactic after another, scheme following scheme. There had to be a way to make them see things her way.

And then, as she pulled into the school parking lot, she thought of the Lord. This was how she let him do the coaching?

*Lord, once again, I've plunged in without checking with You. Thank You for helping me remember You're my Master. I want to do things Your way.*

All of a sudden, it was there. An alternative. A way to show Christ's love without stepping back. She knew exactly what to do. Walking into her office, she placed a call.

"Leave a message," said the voice on the answering machine.

"I just called to see if you had the number for

the guardian angel hotline. I have an assignment for…''

''Sunny?'' Pete answered. ''I was outside. What's up?''

''I'm checking on the availability of a personal angel for this Saturday night.''

''Hey, I'm your man…ly angel,'' he said, a smile in his voice.

She'd known she could count on him. ''I'm invited to a party honoring my father, but I'm pretty sure it's another setup like yesterday. My parents weren't interested in getting together with me as much as they wanted a reunion with Bruce.''

''I was afraid of that.''

''If I don't go to Daddy's party, it will seem like I'm holding a grudge, and I do want to love them— if they'll let me, without putting Bruce into the picture. It would be a lot easier if my personal angel were along to—''

''Say no more. Just tell me when and where. I'll polish up my wings.''

He might not be so willing if he knew the repercussions that might come his way. So far, she'd gotten off lightly, but her dad had the power to make their lives miserable. ''Pete, you don't know what you could be letting yourself in for.''

''Doesn't matter. Angels never worry. We've got the Boss watching out for us.''

She grimaced. ''Thanks for the reminder. In times like this, I seem to forget very quickly.''

''Humans are like that. Angels know better.''

She smiled, loving how his teasing made her feel she wasn't alone. ''After Saturday night, you may wish you had been assigned to Brad," she said, teasing him back.

"Not a chance. His angel has to help him lug that TV camera around and listen to his nonsense."

"True, but does his angel have to wear a tux? Daddy's party is black-tie."

"Hmm, I'll have to check to see if we have that disguise."

The squawk of a seagull, the smell of the seashore, the feel of a new mattress. This wasn't home, at least not the one he was used to. Pete opened one eye, testing the bright light pouring in the uncurtained windows. A gentle breeze wafted through the room, and he pulled the sheet over his bare shoulders. White, uncluttered walls and the quiet lap of water against the shore pleased him enormously.

Meggy was right. Why stay in the Sylvan City house when he had this? Maybe he had been trying to prove that the little house should have been good enough for Lisa. But that was goofy. Why let his life be manipulated by a person who measured "good enough" with dollar signs?

It was time to get this place looking like a home. First off, he'd haul the gym equipment to one of the bedrooms. Second, he'd hire a decorator or, if she were willing, let Sunny choose things. He'd be too busy to do it, but he didn't want to ask too much of Sunny too soon.

For the first time since his accident, he had an idea that couldn't wait. It made perfect sense, investing his insurance settlement money into a building project, and building starter homes for young families appealed to him. Putting cheaper homes on expensive land wasn't necessarily good business, and he might have to build condos rather than houses, but he'd do what he could.

The project would need a name. "Sunny Valley" came to mind. The homes would change the lives of the families who lived in them as much as she'd changed his.

Man, he felt good, waking up rested and…happy. That's what it was. Good, old-fashioned happy.

He tried to imagine himself at a fancy party wearing a tux. No mental picture there. But if Sunny wanted him, he'd be there and try not to disgrace her. He'd keep his napkin in his lap and his elbows off the table. There was something about the way you dipped the soup, and you were supposed to cut or not cut the dinner roll—he couldn't remember which. He'd call Meggy. She'd know.

Pete threw the sheet aside and got out of the bed, filled with purpose. His strong, sweet Sunny had a situation she couldn't handle on her own, and she'd called him. Hoo-ah! It made him feel so good, he could have tap-danced all the way to the shower.

Sunny expected to hear "Alexandra" every time she picked up the phone, but the week passed without her mother responding to Sunny's own message, accepting the invitation, though not the dress or help from Pierre. She'd added that her escort would be the new man in her life, Pete Maguire. Bruce, she'd promised to love like a brother.

That was faith speaking.

*Dear God, make it reality.* If she were to have a

relationship with her parents, she had to have one with Bruce.

Though she hadn't found her dress for tonight, she was shopping again today. She had a basic black that would do, but she'd love to find something spectacular and completely unlike the dresses she'd left in her closet when she left home, most of them mother approved and purchased for her role as the congressman's wife.

The perfect dress, according to her mother, had class and style but was understated so the focus of attention stayed where it belonged—on the man the people came to see. Her mother's idea of perfection, delivered by Charles in spite of her wishes, had been a mauve chiffon creation that she'd already dropped off at a secondhand store. Some lucky mother of the bride would wear a real bargain.

Her own new dress was on a mannequin at the first store she browsed in. It was no bargain, but exactly what she wanted. If it wasn't the brightest, most conspicuous gown at the party, she'd wear mauve for a month. It might not be part of God's plan to brazenly announce her independence with this dress, but at least she would ask Him about it.

And she did. When no bolts of thunder resounded, she pulled out her credit card.

Pete had suggested she dress at his house to avoid Pierre and his assistants in case they arrived as the dress had. If her parents and Bruce stopped by for her, she wouldn't be there. It was a nonconfrontational way of asserting herself—rather wimpy actually, but it was past time she did something.

On the basketball court, she'd always been considered an aggressive player. She could handle taller, stronger opponents and didn't let anyone mess with her mind, but at home she'd taken what her family dished out and come back for more. Of course, on the court, being loved hadn't mattered.

Pete's directions were excellent and she made it to his house without one false turn. It was an impressive abode for a self-proclaimed beach bum, not quite as elaborate as some of his neighbors' homes, but all of the residents of Malibu Colony lived very well.

He must have been watching, for he came out as soon as she arrived and helped her gather her shopping bags, plastic-covered dress and tote bag. Checking her out, he seemed to notice everything from the way the strap of her cinnamon top slipped off one shoulder to the way the matching skirt swished above her knees.

"Wow!" he said, grinning from ear to ear, sending her confidence soaring.

The entry decor was nautical navy and white with a polished oak captain's wheel mounted on the wall and a big brass bell set into a plastered alcove. She wouldn't have been surprised to hear herself piped aboard.

"My dad and I built this place for a retired navy admiral," Pete explained.

"You built it?" she repeated, noticing the fine workmanship.

Pride shone in his face, the kind that came from hard work fulfilled.

"It's beautiful, Pete," she said, happy he had this tangible proof of his talent and skill.

"Well, you might not think so once you see the living room." He stepped aside, hanging her dress in the entry closet.

The living room took her breath away. Obviously, entertaining the neighbors wasn't a priority unless they came to work out.

"I love it!" she exclaimed.

"You do?" Pete's brow puckered above his lop-sided grin.

"It's every jock's dream come true. Who wouldn't like a workout room like this?"

He rolled his eyes. "I can think of one or two."

"Well, I want to try everything." Working up a little sweat was exactly what she needed before to-night.

"Later," he said, leading her to another door.

It opened onto an attached garage. Inside, Old Red sat on the far side, taking second place to a sleek, black sports car convertible with the top down. Its polished surface gleamed under the ceiling lights, a contrast with the lush black leather interior. If she knew her cars, she'd have known the name, for even she recognized it as an expensive car.

"What have you got there, Maguire?"

"A Corvette. Like it?" he asked, wearing the happy smile of a kid with a new toy. "Got it today."

"It's terrific!" She opened a door and ran her hand over the seats. "But what about Old Red? How does she feel about this?"

He glanced at the pickup on the other side of the garage. "It was her idea, actually."

"I'm glad you didn't trade her in."

"Trade in Old Red?" he repeated, feigning horror. "Why, I'd sooner trade in my mom!"

"I take it Old Red isn't the jealous type?"

"Red knows where she stands with me," he said, giving the old pickup a loving nod, "but she's sensitive. She didn't want to risk anybody looking down on us tonight."

Was he serious? "Pete, tell me you didn't buy this car to take me to a party."

He looked away. "Of course not. I was thinking of Red. She gets her feelings hurt when people judge her by her exterior."

Red wasn't the only one.

"Besides, Red's not really what you'd call a party ride. She's more your basic helping-out-when-she-can vehicle. She's happy to stay here tonight, knowing we'll take her for a spin tomorrow."

He was such a good man, and he gave her the most remarkable feeling of safe harbor and peace. She couldn't help reaching up to brush a lock of hair off his forehead. "There's nobody like you, Pete Maguire."

He loved the feel of her hand, and loved what she said, but he wasn't so sure he liked how close to the surface her emotions seemed to be. The inevitable stress of tonight had to be taking its toll. Wouldn't it be better if he could lighten things up?

Backing away, he walked around the car doing his imitation of the John Travolta strut that always made Meggy laugh. "You're not the only one who's been shopping, you know." He looked over his shoulder to see if he'd made her smile.

He had.

"In fact, I shopped so much, my credit-card company called to ask if the card had been stolen."

"That was nice of them."

"I thought so. They wondered why a guy who seldom uses his Gold Card for anything but sunscreen, bought himself a tux."

"You bought one? Planning a life-style change, Mr. Maguire? Going to wear that tux a lot?"

He gave the car's tire a loving kick. "I didn't want to go to one of those rental places. I needed a tux that screamed quality. I don't want to give your parents any reason to look down on you. One snobby salesperson acted like I had no taste when I said I wanted a baby blue tux to match my eyes."

Sunny's heart sank. Her mother would have a field day, making fun of the blue tux, especially if it came with a ruffled shirt.

He tweaked her nose. "Just kidding, Keegan. You looked like you could use a laugh."

She hung her head, embarrassed that she'd thought the worst. "I'm sorry. My timing's off."

"Don't worry about it. I might have gotten a blue tux if they sold them on Rodeo Drive."

Rodeo Drive? That was pretty pricey shopping. "Is that where you got that interesting tie you wore on *Dream Date?*"

He grinned. "Blame that on Meggy. Me, I go first class. Got my hair cut in Beverly Hills, too. Pardon me—not cut, 'styled.'"

"Looks good." Not only the hair, but the whole man. A white mesh T-shirt draped over his tanned, wide shoulders. Denim cutoffs exposed beautifully muscled calves. It was going to be a shame, covering that body with a tux.

"I got chummy with the woman who did my hair," he said. "I told her I was hanging out with the rich and famous, and asked her what she thought I needed to fit in."

"You didn't." She was proud of him just as he was. He could wear swim trunks and flip-flops, and she'd hang on his arm.

"The woman suggested gold cuff links, a money clip and a Rolex. I got 'em all." He flashed the watch at her.

It was an extravagant gesture for a man who couldn't be impressed with such things, judging by the old truck he loved.

"I told her I was going for the suave look, and she talked me into a manicure." He held out his hands for her inspection. "What do you think? Do these look like sissy hands, or what?"

She smiled, as she was supposed to, but it touched her, knowing how hard he'd tried to please. She laced her fingers through his and said, "You didn't have to do all this for me."

Dropping the joking, his eyes swept her face as if he searched for assurance she was okay. She looked at his handsome face—the steady blue eyes under long black lashes, the straight nose and strong jawline, the little scars here and there—and she saw a man who'd never let her down, who'd always try to be there. Pete was so easy to love.

She loved him. Her heart swelled, recognizing the truth.

"I'm glad you called me," he said, drawing her close.

She lifted her mouth, wanting his kiss, wanting it more now that she realized she'd always want him. He lowered his head, his lips coming to her slowly, too slowly. Impatient, she rose and met him in a kiss that he deepened immediately as if he were as hungry for this as she was. She clung to his shoulders, loving the feel of his arms wrapped around her.

When he broke the kiss, their ragged breathing filled the silence. He stroked her face with a fingertip and whispered, "I think I've fallen for you, Sunny."

She nodded, emotion stifling words, but she kissed his fingertip as it stroked her mouth and let her eyes say she felt the same way.

He sighed, rocking them side to side. "You could sure do a whole lot better than me, Sunny girl."

She shook her head against his shoulder, denying the claim.

"Man, I can't even pick a more romantic spot to love you than a garage. There's this beautiful beach not fifty feet away, and we're here."

"This is a very romantic spot," she murmured contentedly.

He looked at the floor. "Hon, we're standing on an oil drip. We can do better."

She didn't see how, but she let him lead her back into the house where he stopped in his tracks. Gesturing toward the fitness equipment-filled living room, he said with disgust, "I want a place to sit down and hold you, and what have I got? A rowing machine or a weight bench. This has got to change!"

"Don't I see a chaise on the deck?"

He nodded, a gleam in his eye. "Think it will hold two?"

She would be surprised if it didn't.

# Chapter Thirteen

There was a butterfly reunion going on in Sunny's stomach, and her hands shook as she put diamond studs in her ears. When she'd tried this dress on in the shop, it had seemed like such a good idea, but could she really drum up the jazz to wear it?

She turned to mirrored closet doors for one last look. Her hair was styled full and sexy. Her makeup made her look prettier than she was. And the dress... Strapless and dripping with sequins the coppery color of her hair, it clung to her curves like a living flame. Sam and Eleanor's formerly pliable daughter would show plenty of backbone tonight.

Stepping onto the balcony, she called, "Pete?"

"Down here." At the bottom of the steps, Pete in his black tux looked as if he'd stepped out of a formal wear ad, only better, for models had the inevitable look of men who knew they were hunks, and Pete's mind was clearly not on himself, but on the person beneath all those sequins.

Pete felt as if he'd been hit with a two-by-four. Sunny was always pretty, but tonight she was stunning. He watched her walk down the stairs, mesmerized, loving the way she moved in that incredible dress. Glowing from her shining hair to her sparkly hem, she took his breath away.

The dress shimmered as she moved, and was so tight, she couldn't have walked if not for the slit up one thigh. As a certified leg man, he approved of that slit. "You look fantastic!" he said, wishing there were words to better say how he felt.

"So do you," she said huskily.

If it were up to him, they'd forget about this shindig and enjoy the evening by themselves. This, however, was Sunny's night, and he'd see that she was treated right.

They didn't talk on the drive to the hotel. He wasn't sure what she was thinking, and part of the time her eyes were closed, perhaps in prayer.

He was praying himself. And worrying, and then praying again. It was kind of a stop-and-go thing. Would he measure up in the Keegans' eyes? These days he had an impressive address and owned a hefty investment portfolio, but he was still a construction worker who'd never been east of the Mississippi.

Still, he was God's child. That evened the scales.

Once he would have prayed, "God, if you're there..." Now he knew God was, and he prayed that the Lord would help Sunny and her family begin a new relationship tonight.

He'd never been to the Crowne, but Bev next door had talked him through it so he wouldn't miss a beat. Good ole Bev, she hadn't a pretentious bone in her body and came from humbler stock than him.

At the Crowne, his first test turned out to be giving the parking valet the keys to his new 'Vette. The kid looked like he'd been playing with Hot Wheels this time last year. Had Bev said to tip the guy now, later or both? Playing it safe, he slipped the kid a good-size bill. It must have been right because he got instant respect, though it shouldn't take money for that.

The lobby looked like a movie set with marble everywhere and trees big enough to grow outdoors. Guests rode an escalator to the second floor, the men in black tuxes like his and the women in fancy gowns with jewels that were probably real. He touched his new Rolex and told himself money didn't make people better.

They stood in a cluster waiting their turn on the escalator. Sunny had greeted several people, but not with her usual warmth, and she hadn't flashed that big smile once since Malibu. Had her self-assurance slipped while he wallowed in his own insecurities?

He couldn't have that. Leaning down as they boarded the escalator, he murmured, "You're sure the best-looking woman here."

She rolled her eyes.

"Well, you are."

"With all these sequins, nobody would notice if I were pretty or plain."

How could she say that? "That is a great dress, but it's the woman that's gorgeous. When you flash that smile of yours, you absolutely light up the world."

She gave him a smile, but it was pitifully lame. "Pete Maguire, that's pure Irish blarney."

If she'd whipped that out in her teacher voice, he'd have been satisfied, but it didn't come close to her usual sass.

"You want Irish? Well, then, Sunny, my love, you're a darlin' girl, a beautiful lass, and that *is* no blarney."

There it was, the full-blown, Sunny-dazzle smile.

"Where did that come from?" she asked, the sparkle definitely back in her eyes.

"Me grandfather, Shamus Maguire, was a boxer, he was. Got knocked out in the ninth round of a fine boxin' match, and never came to, God rest his soul."

"Sorry about that," she said, grinning shamelessly.

"Me own da' said Shamus died happy because he loved to fight and did at the drop of a hat."

"An inherited trait?"

"Well, lass, that's what we're about to find out."

She'd put her money on Pete, Sunny thought, appreciating her Irish angel more than ever.

From the admiring looks he was attracting, she'd say The Face was being appreciated, as well. And why not? The mischievous gleam in his blue eyes, the jet-black hair and his classic good looks combined with a great body in formal wear made Pete a head-turner, all right. Best of all, he didn't seem to care about himself, but concentrated on her.

She took his hand and led them through the crowded foyer. Hundreds of voices vied with a violin trio on a floral-bedecked balcony. It was a wonderful turnout for her father. Through wide doorways to the ballroom she could see myriad lights dancing from elaborate chandeliers and candlelit tables. Behind the stage was a twelve-foot portrait of her father.

"What are we doing?" Pete murmured close to her ear.

"Waiting for one of my dad's aides to spot us and…"

"Sunny! What's jammin', girl?" The senator's youngest aide bore down on them.

"Are you the point man tonight, Al?" she teased.

He grinned, acknowledging she knew Keegan strategy. "They thought they needed my young, 20-20 eyes to spot you, but they didn't know what you'd be wearing. Girl, you're lookin' hot!"

Beside her, Pete bristled.

Quickly she said, "Al, this is my guy, Pete Maguire. We met on *Dream Date*."

"You were on that TV show?" Al asked, a curl on his lip.

"Her ball team set it up," Pete said, extending his hand.

Al took it and visibly winced at the pressure Pete must have applied. Sunny hid a smile. Shamus's grandson was on duty tonight.

Al flexed his hand, giving Pete a sideways glance. "Does the senator know about that show?"

"I think you'll have the pleasure of telling him, Al."

"Oh, no. Not me. Not tonight."

They both knew how the senator took bad news. "Your dad's going to be ticked off enough that you brought a date. No offense," he added quickly to Pete before drifting away to make that initial report.

Another familiar voice sounded behind her. "Sunny! How've you been, hon?"

"Never better," she said, hugging George, her father's senior aide. "George, meet my friend, Pete Maguire."

"Pete, glad you could make it."

She knew he wasn't, but George's faded blue eyes under bushy gray brows seemed just as sincerely good-humored as Al's. These guys were good at their jobs. A third aide ought to show up....

"Sunny baby! Aren't you a sight for sore eyes."

"Hello, Clive." She had Clive to thank for the media stories about her and Bruce, but he could sink lower than that.

The two men shuffled positions, Clive engaging Pete in conversation, so George could isolate her, a tactic smoothly orchestrated, but obvious to her.

"What's with the extra baggage?" George said, nodding toward Pete. "There's only one place reserved for you at the head table."

"Let me guess, between Daddy and Bruce," she said cynically.

"It's time to forgive and forget, hon."

"That's why I'm here, but Pete and I have our own tickets."

"Hon, you don't want to embarrass your dad. You've had a nice furlough, but it's time to get back in the ranks."

"Sorry, George. I'm just a civilian these days."

"You can't be, hon. You're Sam's only child.

Don't hold his relationship with Bruce against him, Sunny. You're his daughter, but Bruce is his legacy.''

"I don't begrudge their relationship. Not at all. I just can't be part of it.''

"Sure you can. You were always a tough little squirt who took whatever came your way and came back for more. I know you, Sunny. You are exactly what this country needs, and this is the right thing to do for your dad. You've got what it takes to be a real winner.''

George should have been a coach. It was as fine a pep talk as she'd ever heard. Too bad she wasn't in the game.

"I see such a future for you, hon,'' he said, waving his hand in a rainbow. "The honesty, courage and wisdom of First Lady Sunny Keegan Daniels will be known all over the world. Children will read books about you. Women will wear their hair like you. People will select you as their Most Admired Woman. Hon, tonight is just the beginning.''

All George needed was an orchestra swelling behind him, she thought, trying to hide a smile.

"Bruce loves you, Sunny. He's learned his lesson, and he'll be faithful to you from now on.''

"C'mon, George. We both know I was lucky to get out when I did. I love my father, but I'm not getting back with Bruce.''

George looked genuinely puzzled.

"But your dad said he could count on you, Sunny.''

She was here, wasn't she? "He can, as far as—''

"That's my girl!'' he interrupted, his radiant

smile all wrong. "I knew you wouldn't let your dad down. He's going to be so proud of you. I can't wait to see his face. Let's get you inside." He put his arm around her, shepherding her away.

She dug in her heels. "Hold it, George! I came with a date."

"That's all right. Clive will take care of him."

"Not a chance!" She shrugged his arm off. "I want a relationship with my parents, but they take me as I am, and they accept the man of my choice."

George's craggy brows drew together in shocked disappointment. "This is going to break your dad's heart."

She rolled her eyes. "I don't think so, George. Daddy's not that fragile."

His eyes shifted ever so slightly, a dead giveaway that he hadn't been honest with her. That was all right. She didn't expect more from a professional spinmeister.

"Let me talk to Daddy, George. I'll try to make things right with him though I won't budge about Bruce."

Nodding, his face a mask, George signaled for Clive to take them inside.

Reproach blazed from Clive's weasel eyes as he guided them to the front corner of the ballroom near the side steps to the dais. "You might think of somebody besides yourself for once, Sunny," he snarled and walked off.

Pete started after him, but she grabbed his arm. "It's okay. Clive's just doing his job. We're supposed to be intimidated."

Sucking in a deep settling breath, Pete murmured,

"I don't know, but it could be he's just miffed because we didn't bring him some of your cheese-cake."

Bruce slipped into the projectionist's room overlooking the ballroom. He ought to be working this crowd who'd paid megabucks a plate to honor Sam. After tonight, he'd need to tap every one of their checkbooks. More important for the moment, however, was a place to hide. His aide said Margo Price was drunk and looking for Brucey. If there was one man Bruce chose not to annoy tonight, it was her husband, that monster Clive.

His aide also said Sam wanted him down by the stage to hook up with Sunny and ease her date out of the picture. He peered out the projection room window, trying to spot her, but the people were practically ant-size at this distance.

"Looking for somebody?" one of the techs asked. "Try these." He handed over a set of binoculars.

From the pirated *Dream Date* episode he'd been shown, Bruce recognized Pete Maguire right away, but the babe with her backside to him couldn't be Sunny…though she had Sunny's bright hair. The woman turned and he got a frontal look. Whoa! He'd seriously underestimated the girl's potential.

His instincts about women seldom failed him, and, for the most part, he'd been right about Sunny when they were engaged. He'd known she wouldn't tolerate him fooling around. He just hadn't counted on getting caught.

Now instinct said they ought to give up on her,

but Sam was obsessed these days, ordering him to "pour on the charm," as if that would make a difference. He'd like to see Sam charm a woman who hated his guts and clung to the arm of a guy like Pete Maguire.

No, he'd sit this one out. If Sunny came through, Sam could take the credit. If she didn't, he didn't want the blame. He'd done his part, providing a stand-in.

Pete watched the large crowd move about the ballroom. "There must be at least two thousand people here," he murmured.

"Daddy packs them in." Her eyes flitted about apprehensively.

If she was nervous, he wasn't doing his job. "What did that guy George say to you?"

"Just the same old stuff about me getting back with Bruce. Now we'll see if I'm welcome on my terms."

Outraged at the position they'd put her in, he said, "If you have to wonder, do you actually care if you're welcome?"

"I care. If my parents can respect me, I want them in my life. The love's not all gone, at least not on my side."

"And if they won't accept you without Bruce?"

"I guess it is just on my side."

Pete laced his fingers in hers. He didn't know how she managed the calm in those butternut eyes. Her parents and Daniels had betrayed her, deceived her and still wanted to manage her life. Yet, here she was, turning the other cheek, going the extra mile, wanting to love them.

Someone or something behind him had her attention. "Heads up," she muttered. "Blonde at two o'clock."

From the corner of his eye, he saw who she meant and felt his blood pressure rise. "Ah, no," he groaned, "it's my ex."

She grinned. "Don't worry. I can handle blondes with one hand tied behind my back." She tugged him toward Lisa.

Resisting, he growled, "What are you doing?"

"It's high time that woman knew what she's been missing."

"This is not a good idea, Sunny."

"Trust me. It's a great idea!"

Lisa glanced his way, did a double take as if something about him were familiar, then looked away without recognition.

"Say something," Sunny muttered. "Talk to her."

He sighed. "I don't want to talk to her."

Lisa whipped her head toward him. "What did you say?"

She'd recognized his voice. There was no escape now. "Hello, Lisa."

She stared at him as if she were seeing a ghost.

"Don't you recognize me?"

"Pete?" She scanned his face, taking in all the changes.

"I was in an accident," he blurted, not wanting her to think he'd had plastic surgery for cosmetic reasons. "Like the caps?" He showed off his teeth, letting her see the gap between his front teeth wasn't there anymore. It had always bugged her.

Speechless, she looked at him as if he weren't quite human. It wasn't like Lisa to be at a loss for words. He smiled, realizing how altogether satisfying that was.

"Pete, you look...fabulous," she said breathily.

He'd like to say the same back, and Lisa did look more sophisticated, but older and harder, especially compared to his sweet Sunny.

"Isn't he a hunk?" Sunny interjected, wrapping herself around him, undoubtedly for Lisa's benefit, though it felt great.

But Lisa had no time for Sunny. "Pete, what are you doing here?" she asked, glancing at their surroundings, silently questioning his presence at a high-ticket, high-society party.

She hadn't changed. He ignored the question and smiled down at Sunny. "Lisa, I'd like you to meet Sunny Keegan."

"The senator's daughter?" Lisa said, obviously impressed.

"It's lovely to meet you." Sunny extended her hand. "Any ex of Pete's is a friend of mine."

Coughing, he tried to cover wild laughter.

Lisa's eyes narrowed. "How do you two know each other?"

Sunny drew his arm around her. "Actually, you can see for yourself. Tune in to the TV show *Dream Date,* next Wednesday. We were the winners when the show was taped several weeks ago. It's been a whirlwind romance, hasn't it, darling?"

Darling? He kind of liked that. "Love at first

sight," he said, snuggling his girl. Thanks to Brad and his camera, he was an old hand at this.

Sunny batted her big brown eyes at him. "You know, Pete, I think Lisa should be the first to know."

Know what? He passed the ball. "You tell her, sweetheart."

"Love to. Tonight, as we drove in from Pete's lovely beach house in Malibu Colony..."

Lisa's shocked expression said that was a three-point shot.

"Oh, you didn't know," Sunny said sympathetically. "Pete must have come into his money after you left."

Lisa deserved a little torture, didn't she? He added, "It happened the day we signed our divorce papers."

Technically only the accident happened that day. The money had come later, but it was more dramatic, stated that way. Maybe Lisa would think twice about upgrading again.

"On the drive in tonight," Sunny continued, "Pete proposed!"

Lisa gasped. "I thought you were engaged to Bruce Daniels."

"Oh, that. Just a media story, Lisa. We parted last summer, thank goodness, or I'd never have met Pete. Pete's the most wonderful, kind, generous man I've ever met."

Leave it to Lisa to pick up on "generous" and glance at Sunny's naked ring finger. His sweetheart had laid it on a little too thick. How would she get out of this one?

"Pete, darling, now I wish we hadn't left my ring in the car. It needs to be sized," she explained. "I didn't want to risk losing a three-carat marquis."

"Three carats?" Lisa repeated in a strangled voice.

Pete wasn't sure what kind of ring that was, but for a reaction like that, he'd buy Sunny two of them.

"Pete, I think Daddy wants us," Sunny said, providing their escape. "Lovely to meet you, Lisa."

Strolling back toward the dais, he glanced back and caught Lisa watching them, openmouthed. How sweet it was, this gentle revenge.

Judging from the glow in Sunny's beautiful eyes, she agreed wholeheartedly. "You liked that, didn't you?" he said, teasing his girl.

"It was perfect! Lisa won't sleep a wink tonight."

"I'm going to get you that ring," he vowed, "first thing Monday morning."

She protested, "Oh, no! Please! I just had to say something that would really zap her. And don't worry about people thinking we're really engaged, not even if Lisa tells it." The words peppered out of her like nails from a gun. "With my reputation for leaving a guy at the altar, we can say I called it off. People will just think I'm a flake. Maybe I am. It doesn't matter."

He couldn't take it, not those words, not that reproach of herself. He tipped her chin up and said sternly. "Don't ever talk that way again. I love you just the way you are."

Those big brown eyes melted. "You love me?"

"Like I never thought I'd love anyone."

"I love you, too."

It was the most precious moment of his life, but that's all it would be, for he saw Sunny's dad bearing down on them. He'd never met the man in person, but that was him, all right.

# Chapter Fourteen

Senator Sam Keegan, professional mover and shaker, approached with his arms opened wide, his face wreathed in smiles. Cameras flashed as he embraced his daughter. Something about it turned Pete's stomach. He knew what it felt like to love Sunny, and this wasn't it.

Flash after flash, the media snapped father and daughter standing side by side, their likeness unmistakable. She beckoned him near and said, "Daddy, I'd like you to meet my special friend, Pete Maguire."

Pete put his arm around her, letting the world see she was his, caressing her shoulder, willing her to feel his love.

"Maguire," her father said, extending his hand, smiling.

"Senator," he acknowledged, surprised at the cordiality.

"I understand you met my daughter on the same television show that employed your sister."

So, the senator knew about *Dream Date*. But why mention Meggy?

"And your mother exhibits her work at the Foster Gallery in Phoenix?"

He nodded, unperturbed. It was okay for a man to check up on the guy seeing his daughter.

"I understand your mother still misses your father, though it's been, let's see, about two and a half years since he passed away. About the time your wife divorced you, isn't that right?"

Sunny saw the pattern and knew it for what it was, a tactic designed to intimidate Pete. But he stood there unflinching, his half smile saying he wasn't rattled by the senator's efforts to push his buttons.

"Sounds like you've been checking up on me, sir."

"Pete," she said, "if I know Daddy, he had a complete dossier on you within hours of knowing you'd be my date tonight. He probably has it all, right down to your shoe size."

Her father smiled. "My daughter knows me well."

"Perhaps I should be flattered," Pete said, staying so cool, she could have hugged him.

"Not necessarily," the senator said, turning his head, dismissing Pete in one swift move.

Behind the senator's back, Pete winked at her. Good for him. She'd seen that move demoralize lesser men.

"Charles tells me you didn't come in the limo,"

her father said, addressing her only, his voice edged with ice.

Sunny lifted her chin. It was her turn. Pete hadn't folded, and neither would she. "We didn't need the limo. Pete drove."

"What? Your Jaguar? Enjoyed that, did you, Maguire?" her father asked with a smirk.

She hated it when her father acted this way. "We didn't come in my car, Daddy," she corrected him quietly. "Not that it matters."

"You didn't show up here in Maguire's old pickup?" the senator said in mock horror. "Well, for the sake of a good tip, I trust the boys at valet parking were kind."

Sunny had forgotten what a snob her father could be.

But Pete reacted magnificently. "I'm impressed that you know about Old Red, Senator."

Her father lifted a questioning brow.

"My pickup," Pete explained with feigned innocence. "Old Red's like one of the family. I'm sorry. I supposed you knew that."

Sunny hid a grin. It wasn't much of a jab, but she'd liked it.

"Maguire, you'd be surprised what I know about you," her father retorted pompously.

"Or think you know," Pete shot back.

"Let's put it this way, Maguire. I know all I need to know."

"I'm beginning to think that's a two-way street, Senator."

When had anyone ever stood up to her father this way? She was proud of Pete for giving as good as he got and terribly disappointed in her father. "Daddy, a person's worth hardly depends on his transportation. Surely there's something more interesting we can talk about."

"There is, but first let's get Maguire on his way. Thanks for bringing my daughter," he said, his smile insincere as he reached in his pocket and brought out a large bill. Tucking it behind Pete's breast handkerchief, he said, "Use this to tip the valet attendant, or keep it for yourself if he snickers at the pickup."

"Pete's not leaving!" she protested, aghast at her father's rudeness.

"Sunny, the man's out of his league here," her father said, signaling his bodyguards who appeared on either side of Pete.

Pete looked at her for direction, silently asking just how big of a scene should he make.

"Daddy! Why are you doing this?"

"I'm thinking of you! Can't you see this out-of-work bum is just after your money?"

Not only was his belittling assessment all wrong, it was proof he had no respect for her or her wishes.

"Come with me," he ordered, grasping her arm.

Resisting, she protested. "Stop it, Daddy."

An older woman, resplendent in bugle beads and diamonds, wedged her way into their group. "Pete Maguire!" she exclaimed. "I thought it was you."

The bodyguards took a step back. Her father relaxed his hold.

"It's about time somebody got you into a tux." She rained air kisses either side of his head. "Harry, look who's here."

Bald, portly, an unlit cigar in his hand, the man greeted Pete heartily. "Pete, my man! I didn't know you were one of the senator's supporters?"

"Actually, I'm one of his daughter's."

The man's quick once-over counted her sequins, but in such an appreciative, nonsexual way, Sunny couldn't really object.

"Do I see a starlet? You want to be in pictures, honey?"

Sunny spotted George tugging on his ear, the signal that said these people had a healthy bank balance the senator had yet to tap.

Her father touched his tie, a signal asking for names.

But Pete introduced them, saying, "Sunny, meet Bev and Harry Sapato. Harry's got a couple of Oscars for producing movies, though Bev ought to have them for putting up with Harry."

"You've got that right," the woman said, lightly whacking Pete's belly with her diamanté clutch.

"Bev, Harry, may I introduce the senator's daughter, Sunny Keegan. The senator, no doubt, you already know."

Before she could respond, her father took over. Charisma oozing, he said, "It's terrific to see you again."

Harry chewed on his cigar, a devilish look in his eyes. "Actually, Senator, we've never met. We're guests of friends tonight."

"Then you'll have to bring them to one of our Sunday get-togethers, and we'll all get acquainted. Have you met Eleanor?"

On cue, her mother slipped beside her husband.

Impeccably groomed, elegant in mauve, she was ready for her job. Her husband had cued her to be nice to the couple. Nothing else mattered, certainly not the presence of one wayward daughter.

For once, Sunny didn't care, not when she had Pete by her side. He caught her gaze and returned it with such approval and love, the feeling washed over her in calming waves.

She must have missed her father introducing the Sapatos, but she heard Bev say, "We're tickled pink to see Pete here with your daughter."

Her mother offered her hand regally to Pete. "I don't believe we've met. I'm Eleanor Keegan."

"Pete Maguire," he said respectfully.

"You're going to love Pete," Bev gushed. "I don't know what I'd do without him."

"Mr. Maguire works for you?" her mother said.

Bev giggled. "Does he ever! Pete can fix anything. I'd trade him for Harry anyday. Not only that, his price is right."

"Bev makes great carrot cake," Pete affirmed.

"But there'll be no carrot cake for a man who keeps secrets. We didn't know Pete knew your daughter, Mrs. Keegan."

"Yes, well, our daughter has so many friends," her mother said magnanimously. "I'm sure your handyman—"

Harry's bark of laughter caught her midsentence. "Mrs. Keegan, Pete's not our handyman! He's our next-door neighbor."

"In the Colony," Bev added, as if she'd recognized her parents' snobbery and had little tolerance for it.

"Malibu?" the senator asked curtly, sending his aide a look that made the man flinch.

"Yes," Harry said, apparently enjoying the senator's discomfiture. "We're all one big happy family out there. Pete, how are those plans coming along for that new development?"

"It's still in the early stages, Harry. But I have an option on a good-size piece of land."

What development? Had Pete been keeping secrets from her?

"Starter homes for young families," Pete whispered in her ear. "I'm going to build 'em."

She was so proud of him, she could shout.

"Bev, it's time we found our table. Lovely to meet you, Sunny. See you tomorrow, Pete." Pointedly ignoring the senator and his wife, they moved on.

Sunny heard her father mutter to an aide, "I thought Maguire was an out-of-work carpenter."

Pete retrieved the money from his breast pocket and stuck it in her father's hand. "I don't think I'll need this, Senator."

Sunny beamed. "Still think you know everything you need to know, Daddy? Maybe you'd better update Pete's file."

It earned her the famous senatorial glare, but who cared? Pete offered her a discreet low-five, and she slid her hand through, smiling at him with her eyes.

Pete was so proud of his girl. She might look like her dad, but she was nothing like the old dinosaur.

"Well, Alexandra!"

Sunny's mother. His hackles rose at the sound of Sunny's formal name.

"Once again you've managed to be quite a disappointment."

Sunny visibly flinched. The cruelty had caught her unaware. Socking a woman went against everything he'd been taught, but he felt like knocking Eleanor Keegan right on her fanny.

"At least I'm consistent," his girl said, raising her chin.

"Consistently irresponsible," her mother hissed. "When I sent Pierre and his people, I expected you to be there."

"I told you I didn't need them."

"Didn't need them?" Her mother looked Sunny up and down, contradicting the claim with a mouth pulled thin with disdain. "You'd cut off your nose to spite your own face."

"Smile, Eleanor," the senator murmured, joining them. "The photographers…"

As if she'd tripped a secret lever, the sweetest expression this side of heaven crossed the woman's face. Incredible, Pete thought. Had she been born able to do that or merely practiced a lot?

"Your taste in clothes hasn't improved." Despite the angelic expression, the woman's voice was dirt mean. "Sequins! Honestly, Alexandra. You look disgraceful."

That was it. He'd had enough. "I have to disagree with you, Mrs. Keegan. Sunny looks beautiful. Any woman here would like to look half as good."

The woman's eyebrows rose. "Pff! What would a man like you know about appropriate dress?"

"About as much as any man, but I can recognize real beauty, the kind that comes from inside, the kind that lifts people up instead of cuts them down. Your daughter," he said pointedly, "is a truly beautiful woman."

Sunny wanted to cheer. Or weep. No one had ever stood up for her like this. First with her dad, now with her mother. If she hadn't loved Pete before, she would now.

Her mother was nearly a foot shorter than Pete, yet she managed to look down her nose. "I suppose Alexandra's garish appearance would appeal to a man like you, but what she sees in you, I can't imagine." With that, her mother stalked off.

Horrified, Sunny started after her. Her mother could treat her that way, but not Pete.

But he caught her arm and whispered, "Let it go. Don't stoop to her level."

Clive Price and her father's bodyguards reappeared behind Pete. "All right, Maguire, this time you leave," her father said. "Sunny, go to the stage right now and take your seat."

"Daddy, you don't want me up there. It would only make you and Bruce look foolish."

"No such thing. Do as I say."

"Please, listen to me. Pete and I fell in love on national television. This Wednesday, when our show is aired, the whole world will know it's him I love, not Bruce."

Her father's smug smile refuted her claim. "I think you'll find that episode of *Dream Date* has been canceled."

Shock registered all the way to her toes. "How?"

"Bruce is taking care of it," he said arrogantly.

"Sam!" Clive interrupted. "Two minutes."

"Sunny, take your place or you'll regret it."

She didn't see how.

"That's enough, Senator," Pete said softly, though his eyes begged for a fight.

"Stay out of this, Maguire, or I'll see that building project of yours never gets off the ground."

"Daddy!" She would not have him threaten Pete. "What do I have to do to make you listen? Write some horrible tell-all about the defection of your celebrity daughter? Is that what you want?"

"You would do that?" Rage glittered in her father's eyes.

No, but it had gotten his attention. "I don't want it to come to that. We're family."

"Your family includes Bruce," he insisted doggedly.

She put her hand on his arm, appealing to the father she'd loved all her life, "I don't mind if Bruce is special to you, Daddy, but I won't be his wife."

"You have to be. Why can't you see that?"

It was like talking to a wall.

"You're my daughter, Sunny. I want you beside me, beside Bruce. The country needs our family. When we care about our country, we put our own wishes aside and do the right thing."

Do the right thing? Had all these years in politics deadened his conscience? Lying and cheating weren't right. Condoning those that did—that's what he'd have her do? It was hopeless. She and her parents would never see things alike.

"I shouldn't have come," she said. Rejection burned in her chest.

"Why did you come? Why even bother to show up if you're not going to do your duty?"

Her duty? Oh, Daddy. "I'm here because Mother asked me to be and I love you," she said, blinking back tears.

Her father looked hopelessly puzzled. "You would show your love by killing my dream?"

"But it's your dream," she said softly, "not mine."

She could see he didn't understand and never would.

"Let's go," she whispered to Pete.

Her father snagged her arm roughly. "No! We don't burn our bridges, Sunny."

"Take your hand off her, sir," Pete insisted, "unless you want this to get physical. People do burn their bridges...when they don't like where they've been and don't want to go back."

The way her father looked at Pete truly frightened her. Men with power like her father could do anything, not that Daddy would dirty his hands, but he knew people who would.

Before she could act, the room darkened and a spotlight searched the width and length of the ballroom. A voice intoned, "Ladies and gentlemen, please welcome our guest of honor, the people's friend, Sen-a-tor Sammmmm Kee-gan!"

Applause thundered. Bleak defeat on his face, her father looked into her eyes once more. "We don't always get what we want. But, this time, Sunshine, I guess you do." Leaning forward, he placed a kiss on her forehead.

She grasped his hand, willing him to feel her love.

Stepping away, he turned, put a smile on his face and waved to the crowd. The spotlight found him, the band played his song and Senator Sam, the People's Friend, strolled to his place on the dais. On his one side applauded his devoted, adoring wife. On the other, his chosen heir.

The heaviness in Sunny's chest had nothing to do with the empty chair beside Bruce. She only grieved for what should have been, not for anything she'd ever really had.

The senator reached the dais, nodded to Bruce who looked into the wings and extended his hand to a pretty brunette who swiftly moved to that empty seat.

Pete squeezed her shoulder, and she clasped his hand. While the attention was still on the guest of honor, they slipped away and walked toward the foyer.

"Are you satisfied?" George called, coming up behind them as they neared the escalator. "Is this what you wanted?"

She sighed. "George, I've said over and over what I wanted."

He nodded. "I know, and you're feeling pretty sorry for yourself right now."

That was a low blow.

"If you knew the truth, you'd understand why Sam has pressed so hard, why Eleanor has been... well, the way she is."

The truth? What now? George just didn't give up.

"We've all been sworn to secrecy, but it's going to come out in a few minutes anyway. I'd rather you heard it from me. Hon, your dad is seriously ill."

She gasped. *Please God, let this just be another ploy.* Even if it was a wicked payback, she'd prefer it. "How seriously?" she asked.

"It's Alzheimer's, and Sam's losing ground pretty fast. Tonight he's going public with it. He's stepping down from his senate seat and endorsing Bruce to fill it. It's a perfect springboard for Bruce's presidential bid."

It would work. She could see that.

"You'll never know how much he wanted you on that stage tonight," George said, shaking his head sadly.

No, but she could imagine. How horribly frustrating for them that she hadn't cooperated.

Emotion whirled around her—despair for her father's condition, sadness that her mother would lose her companion and the reason for her existence, rebellion that they'd expected her to marry Bruce, guilt that she couldn't fulfill their dream. The power of those emotions was a crushing weight.

"How long have they known about Daddy?" she asked, still trying to take it in.

"Privately, we've all wondered for some time. But just before Easter your dad went in for a checkup, and it became official."

"'Just before Easter,'" she repeated. No wonder her mother had called and urged reconciliation. This explained her mother's shrill desperation and her father's urgent reminders of his love.

Tears slipped down her cheeks. Mother would need her like she never had, and Daddy would need to make things right with God while he still could. Lord help her, she'd be there for both of them.

Pete felt so bad for Sunny, he couldn't think of a thing to say. He held her all the way to the car, already regretting the strong stand he'd taken with her dad.

How would this change things between them? She'd said she loved him. Even loving him, would she believe she had to follow her father's last wishes? Would guilt drag her back to Bruce? *Please, God, not that.*

"Do you mind if we have the top down?" she asked when the valet attendant brought the car.

She could ask for the moon, and he'd want to provide it.

But she seemed to want nothing more than a ride in the soft night, the wind against their skin, its coolness dulling their senses, heading for nowhere, just away from where they'd been.

Minutes passed, and his stomach growled. Thinking about filling his belly seemed inappropriate, but food might do both of them good. Since they were all dressed up, he could take her someplace fancy, and he offered. But all Sunny wanted was a cheeseburger and a chance to get out of her sequins. That was fine with him.

They went through a drive-thru and picnicked on fast food in his car. On the way to her house, they joked quietly about christening his leather seats with sesame seeds and spilled fries.

At her place, she disappeared to change. He shucked out of the bow tie and jacket, loosened the buttons at the neck of his shirt, rolled up his sleeves and waited for her on the deck. When she reappeared, she wore a lavender T-shirt tucked into jeans and a sweet, sad look in her eyes.

Wishing he could ease that sadness, he said, "You are one gorgeous woman, Sunny Keegan."

Shaking her head, disclaiming it, she said, "I'm not, but I loved it when you told Mother I was."

Someday he'd insist she stop denying his compliments, but not tonight. Tonight was for cuddling, not lectures.

They swayed in her hammock, her head on his shoulder, their arms wrapped around each other. The light from her kitchen windows illuminated her face, and the love in her butternut eyes made him swallow hard.

"What was that ring you described to Lisa?" he asked.

"A three-carat marquis," she said, smiling. "A diamond big enough to impress, but not so ostentatious it wouldn't look real. Lisa would respect such a beautiful ring. Any woman would."

"We'll get one for you, a really pretty one."

"You're not going to get me a ring," she protested. "It was just fun to see Lisa's reaction."

"But we'll need a ring. I want you to marry me."

She looked into his eyes, not saying a word. *Please, God, don't let her refuse me.*

"I'd love to marry you…" she said softly

He heard the "but," and chill dread crossed his heart.

"But…"

There it was. *Lord, don't let her turn me down.*

"Not now. I'm afraid of what I'd be getting you into."

That didn't make a lick of sense. "If this is your way of letting me down easy, I'd rather you just came right out and said you don't want to marry me." His voice was gruff, but he couldn't help it.

Sunny's heart sank. She'd hurt him. But she couldn't ask him to go through the trials ahead, dealing with her mother, her father, even Bruce and all the inevitable pressures from the media. How could they start a new life together in the midst of such turmoil?

Regardless of the past, she was determined to be the most loving daughter ever. They came as a package, all of them—Daddy, Mother, Bruce and now, even the new woman in Bruce's life. It wasn't something she would wish on an enemy, let alone the man she loved. How could she make him see that?

"If you can't say it," Pete said, his voice cracking, "I guess I understand."

"But that's not it!" she denied, stroking his brow. "I love you more than I knew a person could. But a marriage should be started in joy and happiness. You heard George. My life is going to be a mess for a long time. I can't drag you into it."

Pete closed his eyes and breathed a deep sigh of relief. That's all it was? He hugged her close, willing her fears away. "Don't you know I want to share your life, no matter what it's like?" He lowered his mouth to hers, letting his kiss tell her how much he needed her, how much he would always love her.

And she returned his kiss in the sweet Sunny way he adored, holding nothing back, loving him for all she was worth. That was his girl, his strong, courageous sweetheart.

When he couldn't take any more without wanting what they would save for marriage, he tucked her head back on his shoulder and held her tightly against him. Let her feel his heart race. Let her know what she meant to him.

"I know this girl," he said, stroking her hair, "who's a great one for trusting God." He heard her quick intake of breath. "She's a very lucky girl."

His girl nodded against his chest.

"Not only does she have genuine angels who watch over her, but she has this ordinary guy who loves her so much, he tries to beat those angels to their jobs. I don't think she has a thing to worry about."

"You're right," she said, lifting her head skyward. "Lord, forgive me. I do trust You."

Looking into the stars himself, he added, "Lord, both of us trust You. You've got the best seat in the house. You can see it all. We know we don't have to figure this out on our own."

His shirt felt wet. He knew women needed tears, but he'd never get used to them. Of course, Sunny could cry if she had to, but, please God, not any more tonight.

"I have an update on the story about the little red-haired princess," he said, hoping to dry up those wretched tear ducts.

"You do, do you?" She sniffed, wiping her eyes.

"Uh-huh. You knew, of course, that the little red-haired girl grew up to be a beautiful princess—"

"Oh, Pete, not beautiful."

"I'm telling the story. She grew up to be a very beautiful princess, and one day she kissed an ordinary guy who—"

"He wasn't ordinary. Make him a handsome prince or the story's over."

Man, she was tough, but at least the tears had dried up. "The princess kissed this prince who was extraordinarily handsome." He checked to see if she was satisfied.

The big smile said she was.

"That kiss turned the prince's life around, and he decided to give up his sorry life as a beach bum and build his princess a kingdom called…tat, tahhh… Sunny Valley!"

"Sunny Valley! Oh, Pete!" Tears welled in her eyes again.

Not that again. "The builder—" he said hurriedly.

"The prince," she corrected.

"The prince," he agreed, "drew up plans for nice family homes where kids could play with their dogs anytime they wanted and no kid's best friend was the chauffeur."

Smiling through her tears, she asked, "How many kids?"

"The prince thought the princess should have input on that."

"I just wondered if the kids would have to share bedrooms or if they'd have their own."

"Well, you see," he said, ending the story because he couldn't wait any longer to kiss his girl again, "one of the nice things about the prince being a builder is how easy it is to add on."

"Mmm," she replied, meeting his lips.

He guessed that meant she thought so, too. He couldn't say for sure, not when he was lost in loving Sunny.

\* \* \* \* \*

Dear Reader,

I hope you have a "forever love" in your life, someone to cherish, someone who loves you more than any other. It's a magnificent feeling to have that connection. If you happen to be alone right now, let Pete and Sunny's story remind you how quickly things can change.

They were alone, living in a maze with tall walls that obscured the future. Those walls had so defeated Pete, he'd given up even trying to find a way out. Yet, right around the corner, his "forever love" waited for him in a most unexpected spot. Sunny had turned one corner after another, searching for a way to have a relationship with her family without bowing to their will. Suddenly she had "an angel in disguise" to help her find the way.

God has the best seat in the house, looking down on the maze we live in. From His view, He sees it all. And He knows exactly which way we should turn. Dead ends bring discouragement, frustration and despair. When we remember to ask for His direction, God helps us discover the path to joy, peace and love.

My prayer is that you and I will be great "remember-ers!" God wants to bless us beyond our expectations.

Thank you for reading *Angel in Disguise*. I hope you'll share it with others. If you would like to write, please address mail to P.O. Box 692, East Moline, IL 61244. If you would like an answer, please enclose a self-addressed, stamped envelope or, even better, your e-mail address.

In Him,

Patt Marr

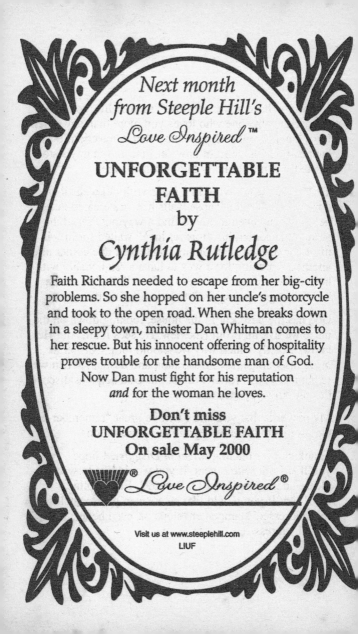